中国经典诗词英译集锦

CLASSICAL CHINESE POETRY

TRANSLATED BY MANFIELD ZHU

朱曼华 编译

商务印书馆国际有限公司

图书在版编目（CIP）数据

中国经典诗词英译集锦 / 朱曼华编译.--北京 ：
商务印书馆国际有限公司，2024.5
ISBN 978-7-5176-1048-9

Ⅰ.①中… Ⅱ.①朱… Ⅲ.①古典诗歌—英语—文学
翻译—中国 Ⅳ.①I207.22 ②H315.9

中国国家版本馆CIP数据核字（2024）第042474号

CLASSICAL CHINESE POETRY TRANSLATED BY MANFIELD ZHU

中国经典诗词英译集锦

编　　译　朱曼华
出版发行　商务印书馆国际有限公司
地　　址　北京市朝阳区吉庆里 14 号楼
　　　　　佳汇国际中心 A 座 12 层
邮　　编　100020
电　　话　010-65592876（编校部）
　　　　　010-65598498（市场营销部）
网　　址　www.cpi1993.com
印　　刷　三河市紫恒印装有限公司
开　　本　710mm × 1000mm　1/16
印　　张　18
字　　数　240 千字
版　　次　2024 年 5 月第 1 版第 1 次印刷
书　　号　ISBN 978-7-5176-1048-9
定　　价　48.00 元

序 言

中国是诗歌的王国，名诗名句浩如烟海，经常被引用的数以万计。学诗、背诗、译诗，是深入学习外语的好方法。与背诗、写诗相比，我更偏爱译诗，总想探寻一条译介中国历代诗歌的蹊径，让中国的诗文化走向世界。

1985 年，在与美国伊利诺伊大学老师和同学的交流中，我就萌生了英译所有我喜爱的中国历代诗词的想法，以便借助其中的名句更好地表达自己的感受，积极参与国际文化交流。岂知，总有比编译诗歌更急的事情等着我去做。结果年华似水默默逝去，激情却难再滚滚而来。直到进入 21 世纪，一家英文期刊约我译介崔颢、李白、王勃、范仲淹在我国江南三大名楼的遗墨时，我才意识到应当立即着手系统英译中国诗词的工作。本册译集的出版，实现了我多年的夙愿。

与其说这是一本译集，毋宁说这是学习和求索的写照。沿着中国诗歌文化的长河漫步，欣赏它奔流不息的浪花，吟咏它传承已久的经典之作，不仅是一种美的享受，同时也在不断丰富自己的文化内涵。译诗也是深入学习中国诗歌的一种方式，反复修改译文所留下的墨痕，则是我不断进取的见证。

借助音韵是学习语言的好方法。借助音韵能加深记忆，并提高学习实效。我国传统国语教材中的《三字经》《百家姓》《千字文》等，无一不是借助音韵手段的启蒙读物。对学习英语的国人来说，这本译集可以帮助他们自修英文，从中英两种语言的转换中体会语言异同的微妙；对学习中文的外国人来说，这本译集可以帮助他们理解中国诗词原作风貌，提高对中国诗词的鉴赏力。

本册译集以 200 余首的篇幅译介，很难做到取舍得当。令人欣慰的是，所选译的诗歌恰到好处地集中了我最想表达的某些理念和情感。

译集以诗词为主体，按照作者生卒年顺序排列。所选译的诗对传递的历史时代信息和诗人的社会处境有一定代表性。除择取了反映社会历史发展进程、极具艺术成就的名篇之外，还选录了一些以往少有译介、评价不甚一致的作品。

译诗须形神兼备。要以诗人的思维方式来译诗，使译出的诗像诗。要注意传递诗词中的艺术气息，注意格律、对仗、音韵等诗词中特殊元素在译文中的再创造。要强调译介的整体效果，要选用今人熟悉的语汇，展示前人的思想情感和理念。我希望自己的译文自然流畅，吟咏上口，有和谐的韵律。为此在诗词英译中，我尽量采用读起来音韵感较强的词作为韵尾。我欣赏“大体整齐押韵”的提法，把读起来口型相似、听起来有韵律实感，但写起来并非同韵的两个词也视为近似押韵的一种模式，如 go 与 girl 或 might 与 mind 等等。

下面举例说明我对译文的追求。在英译唐寅的《我爱秋香》这首藏头诗的过程中，我保留了中文藏头诗的内涵与结构，力求实现内容和形式的统一。用心的读者不难发现，我所译的诗句基本做到了留韵其中，甚至前两行的尾韵做到了与中英文尾韵相同（悠 you / 愁 chou ～ flow / sorrow）。

试比较《我爱秋香》的原文与译文：

我爱秋香

我 画蓝江水悠悠 /
爱 晚亭上枫叶愁 /
秋 月溶溶照佛寺 /
香 烟袅袅绕经楼 /

I painted the blue river slowly and slowly to flow,
Love Evening Kiosk may sense maples' sorrow.
Autumn moonlight shines on the Buddha temple,
Fragrant incense smoke goes around Sutra hall.

我在《中国诗文化走向世界与翻译问题》的论文里（见《第十八届世界翻译大会论文集》），曾具体地谈到诗歌翻译理论与技巧，以及“中国文化走向世界——影响人类未来”等文化“出口”问题，这里不再赘述。

定稿以来，我内心总藏着某种不安，担心对不起读者。每隔一段时间重新审读，总会发现新的不足之处。如“身无彩凤双飞翼，心有灵犀一点通”等很多名句都几易其稿，希望借语感取胜。虽然我知道没有永恒的和完美无缺的译文，但仍希望自己的译作能经得起千百只“啄木鸟”的敲啄。为此，我要加倍努力，力求留下最少的遗憾。恳请广大读者不吝赐教，不客气地挖掘其中的破绽和疏漏。期待此书能在不远的将来再版，以使我有订正和勘误的机会。

朱曼华

Preface

China is a Poetry Kingdom full of famous poetic lines often to be quoted more than 10,000 ones. It is a good method for a learner often to recite some of Chinese famous poetry or translate Chinese poems into English. In comparison of reciting and writing poems, I am fond of translating poems so as to seek for a new way for introducing Chinese famous poetry abroad, which will help Chinese poetry culture enter the whole world.

At the University of Illinois, Urbana-Champaign, in 1985, once I attended a seminar on International Cultural Exchanges, a flash idea came into my mind that it was necessary for me to compile a book or pamphlet with the function of Chinese-English dictionary, which could provide much more Chinese poetic sayings to help me express myself in the international cultural exchange. However, I have always had something else in still urgent need to do. As time goes on, my initial intense emotion or enthusiasm has not turned much stronger until the very beginning of the 21st century when I was told to write something in English about the Three Famous Riverside Watchtowers of the Yangtze Riverside South, and I had to translate different kinds of classical verses written by ancient poets in different dynasties of China. Since then I have written and translated more and more poetic or lyric essays published in an English magazine in China. I was often asked to write or translate some essays with poems that lay a foundation of my anthology of translation poetry. My long dream will come true with the book published.

I prefer to think the book is about learning and exploring notes on poetry rather than a traditional version of poetry anthology. Once I translate my favorite poems I feel as if I were wandering along the Chinese poetry river bank, I could enjoy all the restless poetic waves, reciting the traditional classical poems; simultaneously I could share the lingering charm of human culture and enrich my life. It is a special way to learn from Chinese poetry by means of translation. Repeatedly revising my translated verses reflected my further understanding of their original texts.

It is a good method to fully use the rhyming or tonal system to learn Chinese language. With the help of rhyme, it will be easy for learners to remember some words and expressions effectively. Some Chinese traditional textbooks, such as *Three-Character Verse*, *100-Family-Name Verse*, *1000-Character Verse on Nature*, were compiled by making full use of Chinese rhyming words. My version of Chinese famous poetry could help foreign friends have a good command of Chinese language if they'd like to study Chinese by themselves. My version seemed to be a language-bridge across Chinese and English. I hope my translation will provide some examples of comparison between Chinese and English so as to help learners further understand the original texts; and simultaneously I try to give some concise annotations to illustrate some original texts on Chinese poetry.

The anthology is sorted by the author's year of birth and death. Some of the selected poems with extremely artistic achievements marked a historical progress, others might be seldom translated for they were evaluated in different comments, neither praise nor censure.

It is necessary to have the translation text coincident with the original text both in meaning and in form. The translator should think of the poem in the poet's thinking way, and then the translated poem would be like the original poem without losing important lyric hints. It is still necessary to pay attention to recreating the metrical form, and simulating the Chinese antithesis form and rhythm and rhyme in word-matching way, sound-matching way or sense-matching way so as to win truly poetic effect. Be careful of using current common words and expressions to convey ancient people's lyric feelings and rational ideas. Try to make the translation full of the original sense in a recreational way so as to combine the form with the content, which should be the starting point and stopping point as well as what I seek for on the translation principle and style.

I hope my translation text will be natural and smooth or able to read aloud fluently in harmonious rhyme and rhythm. Therefore, when I translate a Chinese poem into English, I try to select the rhyming word to end a line; usually, it is much better to use a tail vowel as the terminal sound to end the necessary line. I appreciate a saying that a new poem should be "generally metrical both in form and in rhyme". If "go" and "girl" as the terminal sound to end two lines respectively, then the two lines rhyme each other, and "might" and "mind" rhyme, too, and the like.

The following example may illustrate what I pursued in translation. In my English translation of Tang Yin's acrostic lyric poem entitled "I Love Autumn Fragrant", I try my best to retain its original meaning and structure as a Chinese acrostic poem so as to achieve an organic unity between content and form. The careful reader is not difficult to find the rhyming words similar with the Chinese poem. The rhyming word "flow" or "sorrow" is very much alike to the Chinese rhyming word (悠 you / 愁 chou ~ flow / sorrow) in pronunciation.

I Love Autumn Fragrant

I painted the blue river slowly and slowly to flow,
Love Evening Kiosk may sense maples' sorrow.
Autumn moonlight shines on the Buddha temple,
Fragrant incense smoke goes around Sutra hall.

我爱秋香

我 画蓝江水悠悠 /
爱 晚亭上枫叶愁 /
秋 月溶溶照佛寺 /
香 烟袅袅绕经楼 /

I have talked about more points in detail on translation principles and skills in my academic paper "Let the Chinese Poetry in Truly Poetic Versions Spread Over the World" (*Anthology of Theses, the XVIII FIT World Congress*, 2008). Here it is unnecessary to talk much more.

My translation book draft being finalized, my heart is still in some anxiety. From time to time to reread my manuscript, always I can find some new inadequacies. Therefore I have repeatedly revised my translated poems, especially some well-known poetic lines, such as "Without phoenix-like wings, I am unable to fly to you, Two minds think alike, one love road will be easily to go. "

Although I know that there is no eternal perfect version, still I hope my translation will withstand thousands of woodpeckers' knocking and pecking. I must try my best to work hard and leave less regret. I hope readers will continue to check and correct something wrong and to bluntly mine any flaws and omissions. I am looking forward to my book to be reprinted in the near future, so I'll have an opportunity to revise and correct my mistakes.

Manfield Zhu

目　录

击壤歌①

(远古 唐尧时代)

日出而作，
日入而息。
凿井而饮，
耕田而食。
帝力与我何有哉。

The Soil-Hitting Games' Song*

(Far Ancient Times, approximately 4000 years ago)

The sunrise alternates with the sunset,
By day I work, At night I rest.
I drink water from the well I excavate,
I feed myself by tilling the field.
I don't care whether the empire's powerful or not.

【注释】

① 本诗为《古诗源》开篇。这是我国有文字记载的最早的一首诗歌。相传，在远古唐尧太平盛世，人人丰衣足食，击壤而歌。击壤或凿井指的是古人的一种游戏，以土堆或以在地上画定的井字形方框为所击的目标。

* This is the first poem of *Ancient Classical Poetry Anthology*. It was told on the ancient Tang-Yao Dynasty's heyday, the people used to live a happy life and they would like to play the Soil-Hitting Games, singing such a song.

关雎①

(周代 约850BC~550BC)

关关雎鸠②，在河之洲。
窈窕淑女，君子好逑。

参差荇菜③，左右流之。
窈窕淑女，寤寐④求之。

求之不得，寤寐思服。
悠哉悠哉，辗转反侧。

参差荇菜，左右采之。
窈窕淑女，琴瑟友之。

参差荇菜，左右芼⑤之。
窈窕淑女，钟鼓乐之。

【注释】

① 本诗为《诗经》开篇。

② 关关：形容水鸟雌雄和鸣的拟声词。雎鸠：一种水鸟名。

③ 荇（xìng）菜：可食用的水生野菜。

④ 寤寐（wù mèi）：醒和睡，指日夜。

⑤ 芼（mào）：选择，采摘。

Singing Lovebirds

(Zhou Dynasty, approximately 850BC~550BC)

Lovebirds singing show a love show,
A creek goes around an isle to flow.
A girl here looks so gentle so graceful,
A boy seems lovesick with the beautiful.

There are water nymphoides, short or long,
She collects, left and right, up and down.
The beautiful girl looks so gentle so graceful,
Day and night the boy dreams of the girl.

But he failed to have his love show,
Day and night he is lovesick in sorrow.
He misses her a great deal, a great deal,
The sleepless boy just hates his pillow.

There are water nymphoides, short or long,
She collects, left and right, up and down.
The beautiful girl looks so gentle so graceful,
The boy plays a lute to attract the beautiful.

There are water nymphoides, short or long,
She chooses, left and right, up and down.
The beautiful girl looks so gentle so graceful,
Her musical wedding is happy and cheerful.

橘颂①

屈原 (340BC~278BC)

后皇②嘉树，橘徕服③兮。
受命不迁，生南国兮。

深固难徙，更壹志兮。
绿叶素荣，纷其可喜兮。

曾枝剡棘④，圆果抟兮。
青黄杂糅，文章烂兮。

精色内白，类任道兮。
纷缊⑤宜修，姱⑥而不丑兮。

嗟尔幼志，有以异兮。
独立不迁，岂不可喜兮。

【注释】

① 本诗选自《楚辞·九章》。

② 后皇：后土皇天，指地和天。

③ 服：习惯。

④ 剡（yǎn）棘：尖利的刺。

⑤ 缊：香气盛貌。

⑥ 姱：美好。

Ode to Orange

Qu Yuan (340BC~278BC)

Oh, your native land nourishing you to grow well,
Your mother nature can foster you to be suitable.
Your nature has never changed your goal,
You have always lived in the southland soil.

Rooting deeply into the ground below,
You will keep on your unchangeable will.
Your pure blossoms and green leaves,
Look extremely colorful and riotous.

Among thick leaves you show thorns,
Yet you achieve good results.
Either in green or in yellow,
You look colorful in bright glow.

Your appearance is fine, your mind is noble,
Like a great man in charge of a great deal.
You are really unrestrained and elegant,
You are obviously qualified and natural.

Oh, I praise your young strong will to grow,
Your good quality is distinctive and viable.
You are independent not to migrate to go.
Your great ambitions have people admirable.

深固难徙，廓其无求兮。
苏世独立，横而不流兮。

闭心自慎，不终失过兮。
秉德无私，参天地兮。

愿岁并谢，与长友兮。
淑离[⑦]不淫，梗其有理兮。

年岁虽少，可师长兮。
行比伯夷[⑧]，置以为像兮[⑨]。

You have rooted deeply into the ground,
You have broad chest but no greedy mind.
Alone you alienate from the chaotic around,
You are unconventional to go with the tide.

You are prudent and deliberative in mind,
You have not any shortcoming or sigh.
Selfless and virtuous to have morality abide,
Living your life in harmony with Earth or Sky.

I wish to fade away with you as time goes on,
I will be to keep my bosom friends' love long.
Orange looks pretty attractive with no obscene heart,
As frankly reasonable as each branch keep self-apart.

Though the age seems to be short and young,
Still you looked like a teacher, mature and strong.
Your good quality as the ancient prince Boyi,
You are an eternal good example in history.

⑦ 淑离："离"通"丽"。美丽而善良自守。
⑧ 伯夷：周灭商，伯夷不食周粟，宁肯饿死，是后世称颂的有节之士。
⑨ 置：植。像：榜样。

易水歌

荆轲 (260BC?~227BC)

风萧萧兮易水[①]寒，
壮士[②]一去兮不复还。
探虎穴兮入蛟宫，
仰天呼气兮成白虹。

【注释】

① 易水：河流名。在今河北易县，当时为燕国南界。

② 壮士：这里指荆轲。

A Song for Crossing the Yi-River

Jing Ke (260BC?~227BC)

Rustling noisily is the gale, The Yi-River is getting cold,
A brave hero is on the go, He will never back home.
But go to the tiger's deep cave, Or the dragon's sea-palace below,
Look up at the sky to exhale, The breath into a white rainbow.

此地別燕丹壯士髮衝冠昔時
人已沒今日水猶寒

大风歌

刘邦 (256BC?~195BC)

大风起兮云飞扬，
威加海内[①]兮归故乡。
安得猛士兮守四方[②]！

A Gale Song

Liu Bang (256BC?~195BC)

The gale starts to blow, The flying clouds follow,
My imperial power is within the Four Seas,
Nowadays triumphed I back home.
How to have enough plenty of brave hero,
For my empire-safeguarded goal!

【注释】

① 威：权威。海内：四海之内，即“天下”。
② 四方：指代国家。

羽林郎[1]

辛延年 (220BC~155BC?)

昔有霍家[2]奴，姓冯名子都。
依倚将军势，调笑酒家胡[3]。
胡姬年十五，春日独当垆[4]。
长裾[5]连理带，广袖合欢襦[6]。
头上蓝田玉，耳后大秦珠。
两鬟何窈窕，一世良所无。
一鬟五百万，两鬟千万余。

【注释】

① 羽林郎：禁军官名。
② 霍家：指西汉大将军霍光一家。
③ 酒家胡：酒家侍者，卖酒女。
④ 当垆（lú）：卖酒。
⑤ 裾（jū）：衣襟。
⑥ 合欢襦：绣有合欢花的短袄。

Officialdom-Guard Officer

Xin Yannian (220BC~155BC?)

General Huo once had a slave guard officer,
His family name was Feng, first name Zidu.
He relied on General Huo's military power,
To flirt a roadhouse tavern pretty maid Hu.
The young girl was just fifteen years old,
In springtime she had served as a waiter.
She wore her long shirt with an embroidered pair-belt,
With a pair-lovebird picture.
Ornamented with Lantian jade on her head,
Her ears decorated by two rings of alien bead.
As an ornament, her two hair buns so slender,
Nothing was better than her ornamented hair.
One of her hair bun-jewelry worth five-million,
The two of the ornament's worth over ten-million.

不意金吾子[7]，娉婷过我庐[8]。
银鞍何煜爚[9]，翠盖[10]空踟蹰。
就[11]我求清酒，丝绳提玉壶。
就我求珍肴，金盘脍鲤鱼。
贻我青铜镜，结我红罗裾。
不惜红罗裂，何论轻贱躯。
男儿爱后妇，女子重前夫。
人生有新故，贵贱不相逾。
多谢金吾子，私爱[12]徒区区。

Unexpectedly, Feng Zidu, guard officer,
Frivolously came in the tavern to order,
His horse with silver-saddle being bright,
He stopped his ornamented canopy-chariot.
He told the waiter to have a wine order,
She lifted up a silk ribbon-tied jade wine pot.
The officer ordered the expensive dish and food,
The minced-meat-carp was put on a gold plate.
The official guy gave the girl a bronze mirror,
To untie her red-silk skirt in his greedy manner.
It's terrible that you break up my garment,
It's serious that my humble body lightly hurt.
A man loves the new love rather than the first,
I have still loved my own husband better.
Life will alter the newer and the older,
The nobler would keep distance with the humbler.
Thank you very much for your decent manner,
However, your private love is too trivial to utter.

⑦ 金吾子：即执金吾，对官员的泛称。
⑧ 庐：房舍。
⑨ 煜爚：(yù yuè)：光辉灿烂。
⑩ 翠盖：饰以翠羽的车盖。
⑪ 就：靠近。
⑫ 私爱：单相思。

怨郎诗

卓文君 (175BC~121BC?)

一朝别后，
二地相悬。
只说三四月，
谁知五六年。
七弦琴无心弹，
八行字无可传，
九连环从中折断，
十里长亭望眼欲穿。
百思念，千系念，
万般无奈把郎怨。

万语千言说不完，
百无聊赖十依栏杆。
九重九登高看孤雁，
八月仲秋月圆人不圆。

Resenting on My Lover

Zhuo Wenjun (175BC~121BC?)

One of the couple departs,
The two will be lovesick in distance.
Both may wait for each other three months,
Four months, five years or six years, no one knows.
I'm too melancholy to play the seven-string zither,
My eight-line note's unable to pass on to my lover.
In spite of good connection, the nine-links broken,
The ten-mile-long-distance bower's too far to be seen.
I'm missing you for over one hundred times,
With my one thousand time lovesickness,
And ten thousand time lonely complaints.

My long speech's unable to express myself,
It seems to be depressive by one hundred pounds of loads,
I lean upon the slant railing for more than ten times.
On the Double-Ninth-Day, climbing in high spirits,
It's easy for me to look at a lonely wild goose,
In the lunar eight-month, the moon's full again,
But not the whole family members could be seen.

七月半，烧香秉烛问苍天，
六月伏天，人人摇扇我心寒。
五月石榴似火红，
偏遇阵阵冷雨浇花端。
四月枇杷未黄，
我欲对镜心意乱。
忽匆匆，
三月桃花随水转。
飘零零，
二月风筝线儿断。
噫，郎呀郎，
巴不得下一世，
你为女来我做男。

On the fifteenth day of the lunar seventh month,
I burnt joss sticks, holding a candle to ask the heaven,
On the hot summer days of the sixth month,
Everyone works hard with fan, but I'm in cold pain.
The fifth-month red pomegranates meet rain.
In the fourth month, loquat's not in deep yellow,
My mind and heart are full of sorrow, in a turmoil.
In the third month, rivulets gurgle,
Peach blossoms flow.
The leaves were faded and fallen soon.
In the second month, the kite-line's broken.
Alas, my husband,
Darling, my husband,
Next life, I would turn into a boy,
But you should alter into a lady.

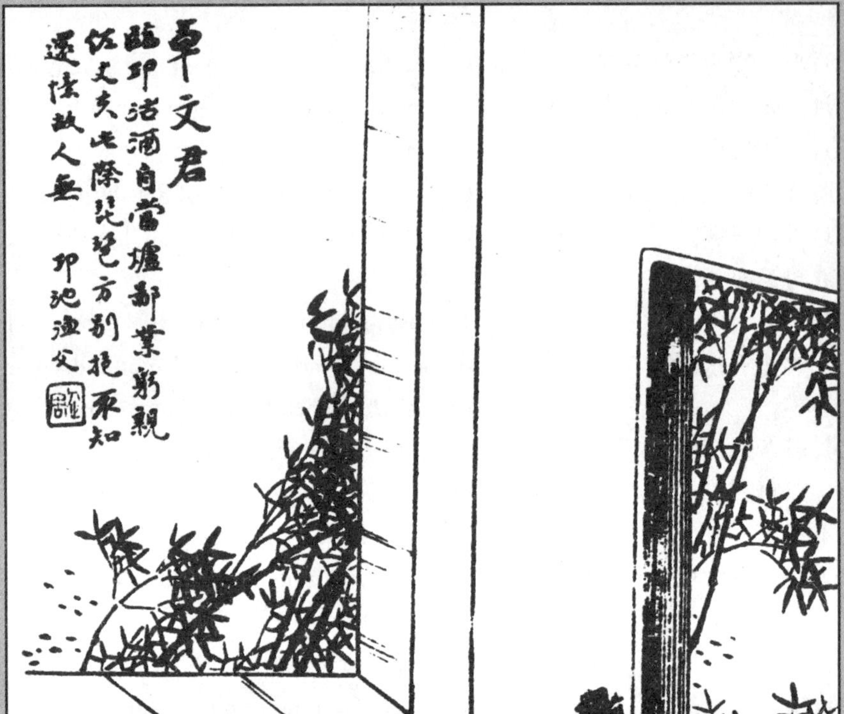
卓文君
臨邛沽酒自當壚鄙棄親
從丈夫也際琵琶方别抱不知
還憶故人無
邛池漁父

秋风辞[1]

刘彻 (156BC~87BC)

秋风起兮白云飞，
草木黄落[2]兮雁南归。
兰有秀兮菊有芳，
怀佳人兮不能忘。
泛楼船兮济汾河，
横中流兮扬素波[3]。
箫鼓鸣兮发棹[4]歌，
欢乐极兮哀情多。
少壮几时兮奈老何！

Ode to the Autumn Wind

Liu Che (156BC~87BC)

The autumn gale blowing away, the white clouds go,
The wild geese flying southward, the leaves turn yellow.
The chrysanthemum is fragrant, the orchid beautiful,
It's impossible for me to forget a lovely pretty girl.
Sailing across the Fen River in a yacht-room,
Wave upon wave, we crossed the mid-stream.
The paddling song heard from flute or drum,
No one will be an everlasting youthful crew.
The younger can never stop their aging doom!

【注释】

① 辞：韵文的一种。
② 黄落：变黄而枯落。
③ 扬素波：激起白色波浪。
④ 棹（zhào）：船桨。

西极天马歌

刘彻 (156BC~87BC)

天马徕兮从西极，
经万里兮归有德。
承灵威兮降外国，
涉流沙兮四夷服。

Speedy Steeds Song

Liu Che (156BC~87BC)

Heavenly steeds galloped from the West boundary,
They contributed a great deal for everlasting glory.
The awe-inspiring surrendered the alien country,
Across the desert conquered barbarian enemy.

四愁诗

张衡 (78~139)

一思曰：

我所思兮在太山①，
欲往从之梁父②艰，
侧身东望涕沾翰③。
美人赠我金错刀④，
何以报之英琼瑶⑤。
路远莫致倚逍遥，
何为怀忧心烦劳。

二思曰：

我所思兮在桂林，
欲往从之湘水深，
侧身南望涕沾襟。
美人赠我金琅玕⑥，
何以报之双玉盘。
路远莫致倚惆怅，
何为怀忧心烦伤。

【注释】

① 太山：即泰山。今山东泰安市北。
② 梁父：低于泰山的小山。
③ 翰：衣襟。
④ 金错刀：有镀金装饰的佩刀。
⑤ 英琼瑶：发光的美玉。
⑥ 金琅玕（láng gān）：镶着金叶的美玉。

Four Lovesick Poems

Zhang Heng (78~139)

One

Oh, what I miss of is to climb up to the steepy
Mount Tai,
Liangfu* blocking the way, it's hard to reach the
top high.
My tears shed as I faced east, looking at her aside,
The Beautiful Maiden bestowed me a gold-inlaid
knife.
Her gift was so precious, how hard for me to reply?
It's too far to be sad,
Why you've lovesickness in mind?

Two

Oh, what I miss of is Guilin's pretty scenic sight.
I might not cross on Xiang River too deep too wide.
To face south, my tears drop, I look at her aside.
The maiden bestowed me zither's jade-ornament,
Only I could reward her a pair of jade plates.
I worry it's too far away to send her my gifts,
My mind's full of uneasy vexation to upset.

* Liangfu is not higher than Taishan Mountain but it can block the way to stop the climber.

三思曰：
我所思兮在汉阳，
欲往从之陇阪⑦长，
侧身西望涕沾裳。
美人赠我貂襜褕⑧，
何以报之明月珠。
路远莫致倚踟蹰，
何为怀忧心烦纡⑨。

四思曰：
我所思兮在雁门，
欲往从之雪雰雰，
侧身北望涕沾巾。
美人赠我锦绣段，
何以报之青玉案。
路远莫致倚增叹，
何为怀忧心烦惋⑩。

Three
Oh, what I miss of is Hanyang city to go down,
Where I want to approach but the road is too long.
Sideways, I look west at her, tears drop into chest.
The Beautiful Maiden bestowed me a marten shirt,
How I could reward by a bright-moon-jewel to her?
The road's so far away that I have to hesitate.
Why the complicated sorrow is in my heart?

Four
Oh, what I miss of is the Pass of Yanmen to go.
However, disorderly swirling is the heavy snow.
Sideways, I look north at her, tears wetted towel.
The pretty girl bestowed me beautiful silk satin,
How could I reward for her a green jade pan?
The road's so far away that I just make a sigh,
The troublesome vexation filled in my mind.

⑦ 陇阪：指陇山。
⑧ 襜褕（chān yú）：对襟的单衣。
⑨ 烦纡（yū）：愁闷郁结。
⑩ 烦惋：郁闷叹恨。

步出夏门行

龟虽寿[1]

曹操 (155~220)

神龟虽寿，犹有竟时；
腾蛇乘雾，终为土灰。
老骥伏枥，志在千里；
烈士暮年，壮心不已。
盈缩[2]之期，不但[3]在天；
养怡之福，可得永年。
幸甚至哉，歌以咏志。

Despite Turtle Longevity

One of <Stroll out of Xiamen Gate>

Cao Cao (155~220)

Although a godly turtle could live a long life,
Still it will be approaching its ending time.
By fog the dancing dragon could fly in the sky,
Finally it would turn dust since it's going to die.
An old horse so tired to lie near stable manger,
Its endless ambition would still much bigger.
An ambitious man even at the twilight year,
His willing heart will not stop beating faster.
Whether your life is long or short,
Would depend on the fortunate or not.
Being healthy and strong with your body,
You will live a long and happy life wholly.
I am so extremely happier than ever,
My poem is an ode to my willpower.

【注释】

① 本诗出自建安十二年曹操在北征乌桓时所作的一组诗《步出夏门行》。《步出夏门行》是乐府旧题，又名《陇西行》。这组诗共分五部分，开头是序曲"艳"，后接《观沧海》《冬十月》《土不同》《龟虽寿》四章。诗题是后人从诗歌的开头取三字而来。

② 盈缩：指人的寿命长短。

③ 不但：不只。

百萬兵南下居然一世雄槊橫
明月下詩賦大江東
卬池漁父畫

短歌行①

（其一）

曹操 (155~220)

对酒当②歌，人生几何？
譬如朝露，去日苦多。

慨当以③慷，忧思难忘。
何以解忧？唯有杜康④。

青青子衿，悠悠我心。
但为君故，沉吟至今。

呦呦鹿鸣，食野之苹。
我有嘉宾，鼓瑟吹笙。

Tune of Short Song

Cao Cao (155~220)

Drink a cup of wine to recite a poetic line,
How much longer will you live your life?
It is like morning dew drops soon to fall,
You have bitterly devoted much time.

I am excited to invite you by wine,
Never forgetting my sorrows in mind.
How can I release my own trouble?
Only you need to drink Dukang alcohol.

Your green collars show you youthful,
I envy you are romantically beautiful.
However for the sake of your talent,
Up to now , I think of you, but silent.

The deer is timid and noisy to go,
While grazing on the wild meadow.
I invite distinguished guests to come,
Let them play their harp and drum.

【注释】

① 行：乐府歌曲的一种体裁。《短歌行》是汉乐府的旧题，属于《相和歌辞·平调曲》。

② 当：对着。

③ 当以：应当用。

④ 杜康：传说中最早造酒的人。这里代指酒。

明明如月，何时可掇⑤？
忧从中来，不可断绝。

越陌度阡⑥，枉用相存。
契阔谈宴，心念旧恩。

月明星稀，乌鹊南飞。
绕树三匝⑦，何枝可依？

山不厌高，海不厌深。
周公吐哺，天下归心。

Hovering the sky is the bright moon,
Which time can I hold it pretty soon?
My worry comes from the sky,
I have no ability to deny.

Passing the field path to meet me,
Gathering together , we crazily happy.
Sharing the banquet to talk the past,
Being hidden in mind and heart.

The moon is bright , stars are thin,
Crows and magpies fly south again.
They hover over the tree three times,
To hesitate to settle down in which twigs.

No mountain hates its heights,
No sea hates its deep degrees.
Duke Zhou is a selfless man,
No world people disobeys his reign.

⑤ 掇（duō）：拾取，摘取。另解：掇读chuò，为通假字，通“辍”，即“停止”的意思。

⑥ 陌：东西向田间小路。阡：南北向的小路。

⑦ 三匝（zā）：三周。匝，周、圈。

七步诗

曹植 (192~232)

煮豆燃豆萁，
豆在釜中泣。
本是同根生，
相煎何太急？

A Seven-Step Poem

Cao Zhi (192~232)

Burning stalks aims at cooking beans' food,
In the hot caldron all the beans bitterly cry.
Originally growing up with the same root,
Why do both of us mutually go to fry?

门有万里客行①

曹植 (192~232)

门有万里客，
问君何乡人？
褰裳②起从之，
果得心所亲。
挽裳对我泣，
太息③前自陈。
本是朔方士，
今为吴越民。
行行将复行，
去去适④西秦。

【注释】

① 这是一首乐府诗，描写了战乱中人们流亡四方的悲惨情状。行，古诗歌的一种诗体。

② 褰（qiān）裳：撩起衣服。

③ 太息：叹息。

④ 适：到。

A Guest from Afar in Front of My Door

Cao Zhi (192~232)

A guest from afar in front of my door,
Asking me “where is your native land”.
I lift up my clothes to go to look for,
Sure enough to see my close friend.
He was holding his clothes to cry,
He told me his experience in sigh.
He had come from the north border region,
Today he migrates to be the Wu-Yue citizen.
Continuously he will migrate time and again,
He may move toward the west of Kingdom Qin.

啄木诗

左棻[①] (250?~300?)

南山有鸟，
自名啄木。
饥则啄树，
暮则巢宿[②]。
无干于人，
惟志所欲。
性清者荣，
性浊者辱。

Woodpecker Poem

Zuo Fen (250? ~300?)

A bird lives in the South-Mountain,
It calls itself woodpecker of man.
Hungry, it will peck wood for food,
At dusk to nest into a hollow wood.
Never to trouble the human people,
What it seeks for is willingly noble.
Glory to such a noble woodpecker,
Shame to birds' inferior in nature.

【注释】

① 左棻（250?~300?），是诗人左思的妹妹，晋武帝司马炎的妃嫔。少好学，善属文。今存诗、赋、诔等20余篇，《离思赋》最著名。本诗是其淡泊自律的生活写照（详见《晋书》）。

② 巢宿：在鸟巢中住宿。

归园田居
（其一）

陶渊明 (365~427)

少无适俗韵[①]，性本爱丘山。
误落尘网[②]中，一去三十年。

羁鸟恋旧林，池鱼思故渊。
开荒南野际，守拙归园田。

方宅十余亩，草屋八九间。
榆柳荫后檐，桃李罗堂前。

暧暧[③]远人村，依依墟里烟。
狗吠深巷中，鸡鸣桑树颠。

户庭无尘杂，虚室有余闲。
久在樊笼里，复得返自然。

【注释】

① 韵：本性，气质。
② 尘网：这里指仕途。
③ 暧暧：昏暗模糊。

My Idyllic Countryside

Tao Yuanming (365~427)

A teenager suited to no lyric poem,
My nature is to love the dune or hill.
Being sunk into the trap of officialdom,
Thirty years ago as an official, I left home.

The cage-birds love their old forest,
The jar fish miss their original pond.
I like to cultivate the south-wasteland,
And keep on toiling in my native field.

My resident courtyard is over ten *mu* in size,
The straw-covered house is less than nine rooms.
The back eaves under the shade of willow and elm,
In front of the hall grow up the peach and the plum.

The villages afar located under the warm sun,
The village market's smoke curling can be seen.
The dogs are barking in the inner passing lane,
In the mulberry, cocks call once and again.

No cluttering dust shroud my courtyard,
My own room is quite spacious and wide.
I lived in a bird-cage-like room, long ago,
Back to the countryside meant to my home.

淵明愛菊
丙寅冬至前一日
企周馬駘畫

敕勒歌①

解律金 (488~567)

敕勒川，
阴山下。
天似穹庐，
笼盖四野。
天苍苍，
野茫茫，
风吹草低见牛羊。

The Chile-River's Song*

Hulü Jin (488~567)

The Chile River, the Chile Chuan,
At foot of the Yin-Mountain.
The sky looks like a yurt dome,
To cover all the prairie home.
Pale vastness is the sky,
Boundless is the wild paradise,
The winds blow grass low,
Easily seen sheep or cattle.

【注释】

① 这是一首北朝乐府民歌。

* The ancient folk song handed down from the Northern Dynasties of China. The author was a famous high official who was good at military affairs and literature and arts.

后庭花①

陈叔宝 (553~604)

丽宇芳林②对高阁，
新装艳质本倾城。
映户凝娇③乍不进，
出帷含态笑相迎。
妖姬脸似花含露，
玉树流光照后庭。
花开花落不长久，
落红满地归寂中。

【注释】

①《后庭花》是宫体诗，又叫《玉树后庭花》，以花为曲名，原是乐府民歌中一种情歌的曲子。

② 丽宇：富丽堂皇的房屋。芳林：这里指高阁下的花园。

③ 映户凝娇：指美女的娇羞容态光彩照人，辉映门户。

Backyard Jade-Like Trees in Bloom

Chen Shubao* (553~604)

Pretty lofty fragrant grove is opposite to the
pavilion.
The newly-dressed beauty is better than all the
women.
Watching the gate, she hides shyness to have no
look.
Out of sedan curtains she smiles to meet the
monarch.
The fairy maiden looks like a flower with dew
light.
Through trees to backyard the sunshine's still
bright.
Whether flowers bloom longer or shorter is regular.
The red flowers withered will be blown everywhere.

* As the last emperor of the Southern Dynasties, Chen Shubao was a fatuous and self-indulgent ruler who was good at writing the imperial verse.

望送魏徵葬

李世民 (599~649)

阊阖总金鞍，上林移玉辇。
野郊怆新别，河桥非旧饯。

惨日映峰沉，愁云随盖转。
哀笳时断续，悲旌乍舒卷。

望望情何极，浪浪泪空泫。
无复昔时人，芳春共谁遣。

Elegy to Prime Minister Wei Zheng

Li Shimin (599~649)

The paradise gate was with a soul-peaceful saddle of gold,
The jade imperial chariot was to pass over the threshold.
In the wild suburb I was reluctant to make a farewell to you,
By the bridge across the river, I used to wave good-bye ago.

On the mourning day, the sun set down behind the mountain,
The sorrowful clouds were going around the cover-sealed coffin.
The funeral music was in an alternative tone, high or low,
The sorrowful banners were either to unfold or to roll.

How extremely unhappy did I feel for seeing you far away,
How sadly my tears were falling down on the funeral way.
Afterwards there would be no such a versatile man,
Whoever would share fresh spring with me again?

如意娘

武则天 (624~705)

看朱成碧[1]思纷纷，
憔悴支离为忆君。
不信比来[2]长下泪，
开箱验取石榴裙[3]。

Wishful Maiden

Wu Zetian (624~705)

Lovesickness let me confuse the red and green,
Good memories let me sad and heart-broken.
Recently I often shed tears, I tell you not a lie,
You could see my skirt's tears stain not yet dry.

【注释】

① 看朱成碧：红颜消逝貌。李白、孟郊、辛弃疾等都曾借鉴武则天写给唐高宗李治的这首情诗而又推出新句。"看朱成碧"成了成语（也可以说"看碧成朱"）。如，李白诗："催弦拂柱与君饮，看朱成碧颜始红。"辛弃疾词："倚栏看碧成朱，等闲褪了香袍粉。"

② 比来：近来。

③ 石榴裙：红裙。

曳鼎歌

武则天 (624~705)

羲农首出，轩昊膺期。
唐虞继踵，汤禹乘时。
天下光宅，海内雍熙。
上玄降鉴，方建隆基。

An Empress Tripod Verse

Wu Zetian (624~705)

Fuxi and Shennong considered as the first ancestors,
Xuanyuan and Taihao were the forefather's successors.
Tangyao and Yushun followed up the above emperors,
Shangtang and Xiayu continued to be the imperial rulers.
The whole great empire was as brilliant as a paradise,
The whole homeland's harmonious and prosperous.
The heaven's strong will let the whole empire mighty,
Initially establish its firm foundation of the country.

游九龙潭

武则天 (624~705)

山窗游玉女，涧户对琼峰。
岩顶翔双凤，潭心倒九龙。
酒中浮竹叶，杯上写芙蓉。
故验家山赏，惟有风入松。

Touring the Nine-Dragon-Pond

Wu Zetian (624~705)

Fairy-like girls touring the hollow mountain
window,
The tall jade-like peaks might see the stream flow.
On the rocky top the double phoenix seemed to fly,
In the pond nine dragons jumped down from sky.
A cup of wine could reflect the bamboo shadow,
The lotuses seemed to be painted on the vessel.
Therefore my native mountain was more beautiful,
Only the wind was hidden in the pine, not to show.

拟小山篇

徐惠 (627~650)

仰幽岩而流盼①，
抚桂枝以凝想。
将千龄②兮此遇，
荃③何为兮独往？

Simulation on Poet Hilly

Xu Hui (627~650)

I stare at sequestered valleys via eyes light,
I touch laurels to imagine the moonlight.
In one thousand years only once we gather,
Oh,why you not let me come as your partner?

【注释】

① 幽岩：幽静的山谷。流盼：转动着眼睛看，指看得入迷。

② 千龄：千年。

③ 荃：香草名。

进太宗

徐惠 (627~650)

朝来临镜台，
妆罢暂徘徊。
千金始一笑，
一召讵[1]能来？

【注释】

① 讵（jù）：岂，难道。

Dedicated to Emperor Li Shimin

Xu Hui (627~650)

Mirroring myself before the dressing table,
Makeup done, I relax to wander for a while.
A million dollars would start a girl to smile,
A call would let me come as soon as possible?

咏鹅

骆宾王① (640~684)

鹅，鹅，鹅，
曲项向天歌。
白毛浮绿水，
红掌拨清波。

Goose

Luo Binwang* (640~684)

Goose, Goose, Goose,
With a long-crooked neck to sing to the sky.
Floating on green water with feathers in white,
Your red-webbed feet seem to stir the green dye.

【注释】

① 骆宾王：婺州义乌（今浙江义乌）人。唐初诗人，与王勃、杨炯、卢照邻合称"初唐四杰"。武则天光宅元年（684年），徐敬业起兵讨伐武则天，他起草了著名的《讨武氏檄》。

* Luo Binwang was one of four outstanding poets or writers of the early Tang Dynasty, who drafted a strict war proclamation to crusade against Empress Wu Zetian (624~705).

風

李峤① (644/645~713/714)

解落②三秋叶，
能开二月花。
过江千尺浪，
入竹万竿斜。

The Wind

Li Qiao* (644/645~713/714)

Release autumn-season leaves from trees,
Make the second month's flowers bloom.
Cross rivers to urge one thousand feet high billows,
Slant bamboo forest's ten thousand bamboo culms.

【注释】

① 李峤：字巨山，唐赵州赞皇（今属河北）人。进士出身，历任给事中、内史、成均祭酒、知政事、吏部尚书、中书令等。
② 解落：能够吹落。

* At the age of 22, Li Qiao was a candidate of the imperial examination. As a courtier, he had served for three emperors in different reign periods of the Tang Dynasty (618~907).

仿朱克正筆意

送杜少府之任蜀州

王勃 (650~676?)

城阙辅三秦①，
风烟望五津②。
与君离别意，
同是宦游③人。
海内存知己，
天涯若比邻。
无为在歧路，
儿女共沾巾。

Farewell to Imperial Service Officer Du Appointed as Shu-Prefect

Wang Bo (650~676?)

The palace watchtower annexed the Three-Qin territory,
The windy mist shrouded over Shu-Prefect's Five-Ferry.
I am reluctant to be farewell to you,
We have had the same official sorrow.
Within the four seas if a bosom friend you know,
The paradise-distance shortens at a stone's throw.
Unnecessary on crossroads to be sad, though,
Still we cannot help controlling tears flow.

【注释】

① 三秦：指现在的陕西省潼关以西一带。

② 五津：这里泛指蜀川。

③ 宦游：指出外做官。

秋江送别

（二首）

王勃 (650~676?)

一

早是他乡值早秋，
江亭明月带江流。
已觉逝川伤别念，
复看津树隐离舟。

二

归舟归骑俨成行，
江南江北互相望。
谁谓波澜才一水，
已觉山川是两乡。

Farewell at the Autumn River

Wang Bo (650~676?)

One

It was in a strange land for an early autumn farewell,
Over the pavilion, the bright moon saw the river flow.
I felt my sad parting idea being lost with the river's go,
At the ferry tree the parting boat's under the shadow.

Two

The returning boats and chariots went on in a long line,
The south or the north shore watched the opposite side.
Who said waters were so narrow just as a river-like belt,
The river and the mountain so near as two villages aside.

回乡偶书

（二首）

贺知章 (659~744)

一

少小离家老大回，
乡音无改鬓毛衰。
儿童相见不相识，
笑问客从何处来。

二

离别家乡岁月多，
近来人事半销磨。
惟有门前镜湖水，
春风不改旧时波。

Impromptu Poems on Going Home

He Zhizhang (659~744)

One

From the young to the old, I returned home,
My hair was grey, my accent unchangeable.
Seeing me, children did not know me well,
They smiled to ask "where are you from".

Two

I had been away from home many years ago,
Nowadays died a half of villagers I know.
Only the home mirror-pool still keeps stable,
Spring breeze cannot make waves changeable.

登幽州台歌

陈子昂 (661?~700?)

前不见古人，
后不见来者。
念天地之悠悠，
独怆然而涕下！

Stepping upon Youzhou-Watchtower

Chen Zi'ang (661?~700?)

Looking ahead, I could find no ancient man,
Glancing back, no one coming forth was seen.
I pondered my motherland so wide, so open,
My tears burst out as I watched the heaven.

春江花月夜

张若虚 (670~730)

春江潮水连海平，
海上明月共潮生。
滟滟[1]随波千万里，
何处春江无月明？

江流宛转绕芳甸[2]，
月照花林皆似霰[3]。
空里流霜不觉飞，
汀[4]上白沙看不见。

江天一色无纤尘，
皎皎空中孤月轮。
江畔何人初见月？
江月何年初照人？

Moonlight over Flowery Spring Riverside

Zhang Ruoxu (670~730)

The spring river and the sea tide merge peacefully,
The bright moon rises up with the tide mutually.
Flowing with glittering waves ten thousands of *Li*,
The whole spring river full of moonlight luminously.

The river meanders around the fragrant pasture,
The moon shines over trees as if snowy flower.
The floating frost seems not to fly in empty sky,
The shallow islet could no longer be seen in white.

It has no dust between the river and the heaven,
The bright lonely moon in heaven could be seen.
Along the riverside who's the first to see the moon?
When the moon is the first to shine of human?

【注释】

① 滟（yàn）滟：波光荡漾的样子。
② 芳甸：开满花草的郊野。
③ 霰（xiàn）：天空降落的小冰粒。
④ 汀（tīng）：小洲。

人生代代无穷已，
江月年年只相似。
不知江月待何人，
但见长江送流水。

Generation after generation, human life is endless,
The moon or the river seems to have no changes.
For whom the moon kept on waiting, you know?
Only we can see the long river never stop to flow.

白云一片去悠悠，
青枫浦[⑤]上不胜愁。
谁家今夜扁舟子[⑥]？
何处相思明月楼？

A white cloud goes with the wind leisurely,
Ashore green maples causes me melancholy.
Whose family will paddle the boat tonight?
Who will miss me to share watchtower moonlight?

可怜楼上月徘徊，
应照离人妆镜台。
玉户[⑦]帘中卷不去，
捣衣砧[⑧]上拂还来。

Over the lofty pavilion the lonely moon in wander,
She should look over at my lover's makeup mirror.
The jewelry curtain could not roll off the moonlight,
The clothes-beating anvil is also full of her light.

此时相望不相闻[⑨]，
愿逐月华[⑩]流照君。
鸿雁长飞光不度，
鱼龙潜跃水成文。

Just now we keep silent and watch the moon
mutually,
I'm willing to share the moonlight with you
happily.
The distant-flying swan shadow light seems weak,
The jumping fish or dragon meant message mark.

⑤ 青枫浦：地名。
⑥ 扁（piān）舟子：飘荡江湖的游子。
⑦ 玉户：以玉石镶嵌的楼阁。
⑧ 捣衣砧（zhēn）：捶布石。
⑨ 相闻：互通音信。
⑩ 月华：月光。

昨夜闲潭⑪梦落花，
可怜春半不还家。
江水流春去欲尽，
江潭落月复西斜。

斜月沉沉藏海雾，
碣石潇湘⑫无限路。
不知乘月几人归？
落月摇情满江树。

Last night the pond dreamed of flowers fallen,
Spring has half gone but she cannot back home
again.
The river sent spring angel to fade away,
The moon reflects the pond light to be tipsy.

The slanting moon was hidden in the fog deeply,
To cross from pole to pole in an unlimited way.
How many people by the moonlight can be back?
The waning moon sheds yearning over the river
bank.

⑪ 闲潭：幽静的水潭。

⑫ 碣（jié）石：山名。潇湘：湘江与潇水，在今湖南。

登鹳雀楼

王之涣 (688~742)

白日依山尽，
黄河入海流。
欲穷千里目，
更上一层楼。

Go Upstairs to the Stork-Watchtower

Wang Zhihuan (688~742)

The bright sun has fallen near the mountain,
The Yellow River is flowing toward the ocean.
To watch one-thousand-mile remote sight,
You need to go upstairs for higher height.

白日依山盡黃河入海
流欲窮千里目更上
一層樓 寫王之渙句
企周馬駘

凉州词

王之涣 (688~742)

黄河远上白云间，
一片孤城万仞山。
羌笛何须怨杨柳，
春风不度玉门关。

Scenic View of Liangzhou

Wang Zhihuan (688~742)

Over the Yellow River afar are the clouds in white,
A lonely city with lofty mountains heavenly high.
The flute singing did no use to the green willow,
No spring wind passed Jade-Gate in the vernal.

春晓

孟浩然 (689~740)

春眠不觉晓，
处处闻啼鸟。
夜来风雨声，
花落知多少。

Spring Dawn

Meng Haoran (689~740)

Asleep, senseless of dawn coming,
I heard birds everywhere singing.
The stormy night made much noise,
How many flowers dropped, who knows?

春眠不覺曉處〻聞啼鳥
夜来風雨聲花落知多少
乙丑重陽寫孟浩然句

相思

王维 (693/694/701~761)

红豆生南国，
春来发几枝。
愿君多采撷，
此物最相思。

Lovesickness

Wang Wei (693/694/701~761)

In the south land, red lovesick beans grow,
The red sprouts develop fast in the vernal.
I wish you to pick up such more red seeds,
They best understand your lovesickness.

少年行
（其一）

王维 (693/694/701~761)

新丰美酒斗十千，
咸阳游侠多少年。
相逢意气为君饮，
系马高楼垂柳边。

Young Chivalrous Men

Wang Wei (693/694/701~761)

A bucket of newly-made wine was worth too much money,
The chivalrous knights were the juvenile in the capital city.
The dude meet aimed at drinking wine for loyal feeling,
The horses were fastened to willows near high building.

九月九日忆山东兄弟

王维 (693/694/701~761)

独在异乡为异客，
每逢佳节倍思亲。
遥知兄弟登高处，
遍插茱萸少一人。

Good Memories of Brothers on Double Ninth Festival

Wang Wei (693/694/701~761)

As a stranger at an alien land, I am lonely,
I doubly miss my kinsfolk on such a holiday.
You climbed up hills afar in height, I know,
You inserted cornel sprigs but I have no.

使至塞上

王维 (693/694/701~761)

单车欲问边，
属国[①]过居延。
征蓬出汉塞，
归雁入胡天。
大漠孤烟直，
长河落日圆。
萧关逢候骑[②]，
都护在燕然[③]。

【注释】

① 属国：典属国的简称。掌管藩属国家事务的官职，这里借指作者自己。

② 萧关：古关名，故址在今甘肃省环县北。候骑（jì）：侦察骑兵。

③ 都护：边防最高武官或前方将领。燕然：指蒙古国境内的杭爱山。这里代称前线。东汉时窦宪打退匈奴的进犯，击溃北单于，登燕然山，刻石立碑纪功。

An Envoy to the Frontier

Wang Wei (693/694/701~761)

The chariot wheels rolled to the frontier side,
Passing through Juyan*, the envoy was to ride.
On both sides of path fluffy daisy seemed to fly,
The wild geese vanished into the Hun's sky.
The Gobi desert's lonely smoking rose upright,
The setting sun was round at the long riverside.
The desolate pass was seen with a scout-knight,
The frontier official on duty's in Yanran Hill site.

* Juyan refers to an ancient border region with two lakes named Juyan in the west-north China.

出塞
（其一）

王昌龄 (698~757)

秦时明月汉时关，
万里长征人未还。
但使龙城飞将[①]在，
不教胡马度阴山[②]。

Go to the Frontier

Wang Changling (698~757)

Over the Han's border was the bright moon of Qin,
Guardsmen of the Great Wall did not triumph to return.
If the flying General Li on duty of the Dragon-City region,
Hun's cavalry dared not to cross the Yin-Mountain.

【注释】

① 龙城：匈奴祭天集会的地方。飞将：指汉朝名将李广，匈奴称他为“飞将军”。
② 阴山：昆仑山的北支，是我国北方的屏障。

静夜思

李白 (701~762)

床前明月光，
疑是地上霜。
举头望明月，
低头思故乡。

Homesick at Quiet Night

Li Bai (701~762)

My bed is full of the bright moonlight,
Is it the frost painting ground in white?
Looking up at the moon being bright,
Looking down with the homesick mind.

望庐山瀑布

李白 (701~762)

日照香炉生紫烟[1]，
遥看瀑布挂前川。
飞流直下三千尺[2]，
疑是银河落九天。

Looking up at Lushan Waterfall

Li Bai (701~762)

Over Burner-peak mist rises in the sunshine,
On the hillside, a waterfall is lying high.
The three thousand feet long waterfall seems to fly,
Is the Milky Way falling from the sky?

【注释】

① 香炉：指庐山的香炉峰。紫烟：指日光透过云雾，远望如紫色的烟云。

② 三千尺：形容山高，夸张说法。

塞下曲
（六首之一）

李白 (701~762)

五月天山雪，无花只有寒。
笛中闻折柳，春色未曾看。
晓战随金鼓，宵眠抱玉鞍。
愿将腰下剑，直为斩楼兰。

One of the Selected Frontier Songs

Li Bai (701~762)

May snow, the Tianshan Mountains hold,
That left no flower blossoming but cold.
The flute playing a melody of Weeping Willow,
No vernal scene could be seen on any road.
The beating drum broke out the dawn-battle,
At night, knights were sleeping on their saddle.
At any time, they desire to pull their sword out,
In order to kill Loulan Kingdom foes at all.

赠汪伦

李白 (701~762)

李白乘舟将欲行，
忽闻岸上踏歌声。
桃花潭水深千尺，
不及汪伦送我情。

Dedicated to Wang Lun

Li Bai (701~762)

Poet Li Bai was boarding a boat to go,
At once he heard of a song ashore to follow.
The Peach Blossom Lake was one thousand feet deep,
Not as deep as Wang Lun's true friendship.

怨情

李白 (701~762)

美人卷珠帘，
深坐颦[①]蛾眉。
但见泪痕湿，
不知心恨谁。

A Girl's Plaint

Li Bai (701~762)

Rolling up her bead-stringed curtain,
She sat frowning with lonely emotion.
The trace of her tears could be seen,
She had no idea to hate the exact man.

【注释】

① 深坐：长久的坐。颦（pín）：皱眉。

月下独酌
（四首其一）

李白 (701~762)

花间一壶酒，
独酌无相亲。
举杯邀明月，
对影成三人。
月既不解饮，
影徒随我身。
暂伴月将影，
行乐须及春。

我歌月徘徊，
我舞影零乱。
醒时同交欢，
醉后各分散。
永结无情游，
相期邈云汉。

Drinking Alone under the Moon

Li Bai (701~762)

A pot of wine on flowers' shadow,
I drink without a friend follow.
I raise my cup to Moon as a fellow,
Three men are Moon and I and shadow.
Moon drinks no wine of my sorrow,
Merely my shadow is to follow.
As a timely partner of Moon with shadow,
I seek for pleasure before being old.

I sing with Moon to ramble,
I dance with disordered shadow.
Sober, we are cheerful,
Drunk, we are separable.
Alas, we are of everlasting passionate pal,
Let's reunite at the Milky Way as our goal.

登金陵凤凰台

李白 (701~762)

凤凰台上凤凰游，
凤去台空江自流。
吴宫花草埋幽径，
晋代衣冠成古丘。
三山半落青天外，
二水中分白鹭洲。
总为浮云能遮日，
长安不见使人愁。

The Phoenix Rampart at Jinling

Li Bai (701~762)

Over the phoenix rampart the phoenix in travel,
The phoenix flying away, left the river alone to
flow.
The Wu-palace's grass and flower covered gloomy
path,
The Jin-crown was buried in a mound of the
death.
Three peaks half-fallen beyond the blue sky,
The Egret Islet divides the river to pass by.
Always I worry floating clouds cover the sun,
And think of no Capital City Chang'an seen.

鹦鹉洲

李白 (701~762)

鹦鹉东过吴江水，
江上洲传鹦鹉名。
鹦鹉西飞陇山去，
芳洲之树何青青。
烟开兰叶香风暖，
岸夹桃花锦浪生。
迁客此时徒极目，
长洲孤月向谁明？

The Parrot Islet

Li Bai (701~762)

Before a parrot has flown the Islet,
The islet lying in the river called Parrot.
A parrot flew west over Long Mountain,
The fragrant islet's trees luxuriantly green.
The mist seems to be in bloom in the fragrant air,
The riverbanks' peach blossoms like wave flower.
The passengers look at the remote scenery sight,
They wonder for whom the moon shining so bright.

秋浦歌

（十七首之一）

李白 (701~762)

白发三千丈，
缘愁似个长。
不知明镜里，
何处得秋霜。

Autumn Riverside

Li Bai (701~762)

My gray hair grew up three-thousand-*Zhang**,
Due to my sorrows had lasted too much long.
I don't know which day the mirror was so bright,
That had my temple hair dyed in frosty white.

* *Zhang*（丈）is a unit of length of China, which equals to three and one third meters.

行路难

（其一）

李白 (701~762)

金樽清酒斗十千，
玉盘珍馐直万钱。
停杯投箸不能食，
拔剑四顾心茫然。

欲渡黄河冰塞川，
将登太行雪暗天。
闲来垂钓坐溪上，
忽复乘舟梦日边。

行路难，行路难，
多歧路，今安在。
长风破浪会有时，
直挂云帆济沧海。

It's Hard on the Go

Li Bai (701~762)

A gold bucket of pure wine is worth precious,
More precious is a jade disk of food delicious.
It's impossible for me to order such drink or food,
Sword out of sheath I look around in dazed mood.

Crossing the Yellow River, ice stopped passing by,
Climbing up Mt. Taihang, snow darkened the sky.
Aboard sitting on the creek for fishing leisurely,
The boat carried my dream to the sun suddenly.

I am on the go, step by step, harder and harder,
There are more crossroads to meet more danger.
The long wind had a chance to ride the crazy
billow,
The cloud-like sail would cross the vast ocean to
flow.

将进酒[1]

李白 (701~762)

君不见黄河之水天上来，
奔流到海不复回。
君不见高堂明镜悲白发，
朝如青丝暮成雪。
人生得意须尽欢，
莫使金樽空对月。
天生我材必有用，
千金散尽还复来。
烹羊宰牛且为乐，
会须一饮三百杯。
岑夫子，丹丘生[2]，
将进酒，杯莫停。

【注释】

① 这是一首乐府诗。

② 岑夫子：指岑勋，李白的朋友。丹丘生：指元丹丘，李白的朋友。

Urge to Drink

Li Bai (701~762)

Don't you see the Yellow River flying from the
heavenly sky?
Never going back until rushing currently fast to
the seaside.
Don't you see my hair gray in my chamber hall's
mirror inside?
It was one night before my hair had turned white.
Alas, be pleased to enjoy yourself in time in life,
Cheer to the moon, and fill in your cup of wine.
I was born genius, surely to be employed with luck,
Much gold cash run out, more money would be
back.
Cooking a whole body of sheep was just for fun,
It might be necessary to drink three hundred cupfuls
of wine.
Toast to Scholar Cen, toast to Dan Qiu,
Urge them to drink series of cups in a line.

与君歌一曲，
请君为我侧耳听。
钟鼓馔玉不足贵，
但愿长醉不愿醒。
古来圣贤皆寂寞，
惟有饮者留其名。
陈王昔时宴平乐[③]，
斗酒十千恣欢谑。
主人何为言少钱，
径须沽取对君酌。
五花马，千金裘，
呼儿将出换美酒，
与尔同销万古愁。

I would like to sing a song together with you,
Please listen to me carefully for my own show.
It's not valued for bells, drums and jewelry,
But long sleep after drink is full of much joy.
All the ancient scholarly elites were lonely,
Only tipplers' fame will ever last eternally.
Once Cao Zhi gave a banquet in Pingle Temple,
Luxuriously he ordered precious wine on the table.
Unnecessary for the host to worry in shortage of money,
It is necessary for me to drink to you directly and freely.
My flowery-dappled horse or priceless fur robe with jewelry,
Could be changed for good wine, help me order, my boy,
I'll release all of my eternal sorrows with you anyway.

③ 陈王：指陈思王曹植。平乐：宫殿名，即平乐观。位于洛阳西门外，是汉代达官显贵的娱乐场所。

太白醉酒
邛池漁父畫於滬上

关山月①

李白 (701~762)

明月出天山②，
苍茫云海间。
长风几万里，
吹度玉门关。

汉下③白登道，
胡窥青海湾。
由来征战地，
不见有人还。

戍客望边色，
思乡多苦颜。
高楼当此夜，
叹息未应闲。

The Moon over the Mountain Pass

Li Bai (701~762)

The moon had risen up from the Tianshan Mountain,
Hazily she was lying back on the cloudy ocean.
The wind was blowing thousands of miles long,
Through the Yumen-Pass to be going on.

The Han-army marched on to the Baideng Way,
The Hun foes glimpsed at Qinghai Bay.
The ancient battlefield was coveted to control,
But no soldier could be seen to return home.

I am looking at the frontier sight-seeing,
Homesick fighters were never smiling.
Being homesick of love chamber's family,
At night they were quietly to sigh restlessly.

【注释】

① 关山月：古乐府诗题，作品大多抒发离别哀伤之情。

② 天山：指祁连山。

③ 下：指出兵。

苏台[1]怀古

李白 (701~762)

旧苑荒台杨柳新，
菱歌清唱不胜春。
只今唯有西江月，
曾照吴王宫里人。

【注释】

① 苏台：即姑苏台，始建于吴王阖闾，夫差继位后，又加以整修。越国攻败吴国时，姑苏台被焚，变为废墟。

Ode to an Ancient Gusu Imperial Watchtower

Li Bai (701~762)

The ancient imperial watchtower willows fresh
  anew,
The water chestnut song is not better than the
  vernal.
Nowadays it is only the west-river's moon so
  bright,
That silently shone to Wu King's Queen at night.

舊苑荒臺楊柳新菱歌清唱
不勝春只今惟有西江月曾
照吳王宮裏人 寫李青蓮句
卯池漁父寫於海上一粟浮家

与夏十二登岳阳楼

李白（701~762）

楼观岳阳尽，川迴洞庭开。
雁引愁心去，山衔好月来。
云间连下榻，天上接行杯。
醉后凉风起，吹人舞袖回。

Go Upstairs to Yueyang Watchtower with Xia Shier

Li Bai (701~762)

On watchtower you could see the Yueyang panoramic,
The silent river's zigzagging around the Dongting Lake.
The wild geese attracted my sorrowful mind away,
The full moon was kissed by the mountain naturally.
The floating clouds entering our staying room,
The heaven would share wine of the bosom.
After they tipsy, the cool wind started to blow,
And promote the bosom friends to go home.

早发白帝城

李白 (701~762)

朝辞白帝彩云间，
千里江陵一日还。
两岸猿声啼不住，
轻舟已过万重山。

Early Morning Starting off from Baidi City's Colorful Clouds

Li Bai (701~762)

The boat started off from Baidi City's morning sunlight,
It took just a day to reach Jiangling at Yangtze Riverside.
Along both river banks monkeys cried time and again,
My light boat fast scanned ten thousand layers of mountain.

黄鹤楼

崔颢 (704~754)

昔人已乘黄鹤去，
此地空余黄鹤楼。
黄鹤一去不复返，
白云千载空悠悠。
晴川历历汉阳树，
芳草萋萋鹦鹉洲。
日暮乡关何处是，
烟波江上使人愁。

The Yellow Crane Tower

Cui Hao (704~754)

Long ago a man riding a yellow crane flew away,
The Yellow Crane Tower was left empty till today.
The yellow crane had never returned once again,
The one thousand year lonely clouds leisurely
remain.
The river was so clear to mirror the tree shadow,
The grasses on the Parrot Islet luxuriantly grow.
The sun in the twilight, I am on my way home,
The mist-covered river flowed with my sorrow.

别董大

高适 (704~765)

千里黄云白日曛，
北风吹雁雪纷纷。
莫愁前路无知己，
天下谁人不识君。

Farewell to Dong Da

Gao Shi (704~765)

The sun in dimly white, the one thousand *li* clouds in yellow,
The cold wind blows the wild geese in drifting snow.
Don't worry that there is no bosom friend ahead of road,
All over the world, no people have not known you.

千里黃雲白日曛北風
吹雁雪紛紛莫愁前路
無知己天下誰人不識君
寫高適句

塞上听吹笛

高适 (704~765)

雪净胡天牧马还，
月明羌笛戍楼间。
借问梅花何处落，
风吹一夜满关山。

Listening to the Frontier Flute

Gao Shi (704~765)

Treading clear snow, herdsmen returned home,
The moon over watchtower I heard of a flute tone.
Where were the plum blossoms falling down?
Just a night they spread over the whole ground.

塞下曲
（其一）

常建 (708~765)

玉帛朝回望帝乡，
乌孙[1]归去不称王。
天涯静处无征战，
兵气销为日月光。

A Song Beyond the Border

Chang Jian (708~765)

Offering tribute and reluctantly leaving the Capital
for home,
Wu Sun submitted to the emperor not to establish
any kingdom.
At the edge of the empire, the tribe was peaceful
everywhere,
Warring spirit altered to bright sunshine in harmony
atmosphere.

【注释】

① 乌孙：汉代连接东西方草原交通的最重要民族之一。

劝学诗

颜真卿 (709~784)

三更灯火五更鸡，
正是男儿读书时。
黑发不知勤学早，
白首方悔读书迟。

Encouraging Learning

Yan Zhenqing (709~784)

After midnight cocks would call for daybreak,
It is time that boys ought to read their book.
Childish kids don't know for diligent study early,
Learning would be too late until their hair's gray.

月夜忆舍弟

杜甫 (712~770)

戍鼓断人行，边秋一雁声。
露从今夜白，月是故乡明。
有弟皆分散，无家问死生。
寄书长不达，况乃未休兵。

Under the Moonlight Recalling My Younger Brother

Du Fu (712~770)

The night drum-timer limited man's walking,
The autumn frontier wild geese flied, sighing.
Cold dews start to be white from tonight,
Only hometown's moon was extremely bright.
My brother far from me separated outside,
No home news told whether he lived or died.
He used hardly to receive any letter of mine,
For the war was still on the battlefield line.

咏怀古迹[①]

（五首之三）

杜甫 (712~770)

群山万壑赴荆门，
生长明妃[②]尚有村。
一去紫台连朔漠，
独留青冢向黄昏。
画图省识[③]春风面，
环佩空归夜月魂。
千载琵琶作胡语，
分明怨恨曲中论。

【注释】

①《咏怀古迹五首》是杜甫于公元766年在夔州和自夔州赴江陵途中所写的一组七言律诗。本诗为第三首，是杜甫路过昭君村时所作。

② 明妃：指王昭君。

③ 省识：未能详察。因为汉元帝昏庸，“按图召幸”，故而辨识不出美恶真相，才害得昭君遗恨终身。

A Memorial Poem to an Ancient Beauty Wang Zhaojun

Du Fu (712~770)

Myriad valleys were spreading to the hilly Jingmen Gate,
The imperial concubine's born in an adjacent hamlet.
The Violet Palace situated in the vast desert of Hun,
Her Green-Tomb was lonely to face the setting sun.
Her beauty couldn't be sensed due to painter's evil,
She dreamed of home in her pure moonlight soul.
As the Hun's tongue, her *Pipa* played one thousand year long,
That's her clearly everlasting plaint-and-hatred song.

王昭君
抱得琵琶不忍彈胡沙獵々雪漫々
曉來馬上寒如許信是將軍出塞難
丙寅蒲節後五日企周畫於燈下

绝句

杜甫 (712~770)

王杨卢骆[1]当时体，
轻薄为文哂未休。
尔曹身与名俱灭，
不废江河万古流。

Heptasyllabic Quatrain

Du Fu (712~770)

Wang, Yang, Lu and Luo created timely style of
poetry,
The superficial critics were mockery of the four
endlessly.
All the commentators lost face to be shameful,
None of them could stop rivers eternally to flow.

【注释】

① 王勃、杨炯、卢照邻、骆宾王并称“初唐四杰”。

绝句

杜甫 (712~770)

两个黄鹂鸣翠柳，
一行白鹭上青天。
窗含西岭千秋雪，
门泊东吴万里船。

Heptasyllabic Quatrain

Du Fu (712~770)

Two yellow orioles were singing in the green willow,
A flock of white egrets were flying into the blue sky.
West-Ridge heavy snow was swallowed by my window,
East-Wu myriad ships sailed to pass my door nearby.

春望

杜甫 (712~770)

国破山河在，城春草木深。
感时花溅泪，恨别鸟惊心。
烽火连三月，家书抵万金。
白头搔更短，浑欲不胜簪。

Spring View

Du Fu (712~770)

The country broken but mountains and rivers remain,
The city is overgrown with weeds in spring.
Sensational of situation, even flowers are tearful heavily,
Hateful of farewell, even birds feel uneasy surprisingly.
The warring flames have lasted for three months long,
The letter is worth myriad gold from my hometown.
My grcy hair turned thinner and shorter,
It is impossible to hold my hairpin tighter.

碛中作[1]

岑参 (715~770)

走马[2]西来欲到天，
辞家见月两回圆。
今夜未知何处宿，
平沙[3]莽莽绝人烟。

A Flash Idea Came in Mind from the Desert

Cen Shen (715~770)

Riding to the West frontier seems to the Heaven,
Since my leaving home, the full moon twice seen.
I wonder where I will be staying tonight,
As the flat desert vast without human sight.

【注释】

① 碛（qì）：沙石地，沙漠。

② 走马：骑马疾走。

③ 平沙：平坦广阔的沙漠。

白雪歌送武判官归京

岑参 (715~770)

北风卷地白草折，
胡天①八月即飞雪。
忽如一夜春风来，
千树万树梨花开。
散入珠帘湿罗幕，
狐裘不暖锦衾薄。
将军角弓不得控，
都护铁衣②冷难着。
瀚海阑干③百丈冰，
愁云惨淡万里凝。
中军置酒饮归客，
胡琴琵琶与羌笛。
纷纷暮雪下辕门④，
风掣红旗冻不翻。

【注释】

① 胡天：塞北的天空。

② 铁衣：铠甲。

③ 阑干：纵横交错的样子。

④ 辕门：军营的门。

A Snowing Song to an Army Officer Back to the Capital

Cen Shen (715~770)

The north wind rolling up with broken grasses in white,
Even in August, the snow was flying in the Hun's sky.
As if spring breeze suddenly came to blow one night,
To have thousands of pear trees blooming in white.
Through bead curtains, the snow got our tent wet,
Fox fur coat or thick quilt could not stop the cold.
The cold snow got General unskillful to draw his bow,
It was hard for Duhu-officer to put on his cold coat.
The vast Gobi desert was covered by heavy icy snow,
Even the clouds seemed to be gloomy with the cold.
At headquarters going on was the farewell party show,
Musical instrument *Huqin*, *Pipa* or flute in play.
The falling snow covered the tent at the door way,
The red banner could hardly flutter with snowy day.

轮台东门送君去， 去时雪满天山路。 山回路转不见君， 雪上空留马行处。	To Luntai's east gate to wave good-bye to you, I saw snow cover the Tianshan Mountain road. Your shadow along the zigzag path with snow, There's nothing but horses' footprint below.

枫桥夜泊

张继 (生卒年不详)

月落乌啼霜满天，
江枫渔火对愁眠。
姑苏城外寒山寺，
夜半钟声到客船。

Mooring by Maple Bridge at Night

Zhang Ji (birth and death unknown)

The moon lost in the frosty sky, lonely dusk crows
cried,
Sleepless, I watched red maples and fishing light.
The Cold-Hill Temple located in City Gusu's outside,
The boat passengers heard the bell at midnight.

滁州西涧[1]

韦应物 (生卒年不详)

独怜幽草涧边生，
上有黄鹂深树鸣。
春潮带雨晚来急，
野渡无人舟自横。

The West Valley Stream in Chuzhou County

Wei Yingwu (birth and death unknown)

It's a pity I watch lonely grass in the canyon grow,
The grove depth heard of singing orioles in
　yellow.
The spring late tide with rain rolling on urgently,
At the wild ferry nobody paddled a boat away.

【注释】

① 滁州：在今安徽滁州。西涧：在滁州城西，俗名称上马河。

獨憐幽草澗邊生上有黃鸝
深樹鳴春潮帶雨晚來急
野渡無人舟自横
邛池漁父寫韋應物句

塞下曲

卢纶 (739~799)

月黑雁飞高，
单于夜遁逃。
欲将轻骑逐，
大雪满弓刀。

A Frontier Poem

Lu Lun (739~799)

The moon being dim, the wild geese flying high,
The Hun’s knights were quietly to flee at night.
The frontier army tried to drive all of the foes,
Their bows or swords covered by big snow.

边思

李益 (746~829)

腰垂锦带佩吴钩[①]，
走马曾防玉塞[②]秋。
莫笑关西[③]将家子，
只将诗思入凉州。

【注释】

① 吴钩：一种吴地出产的弯刀。杜甫诗有“少年别有赠，含笑看吴钩”之句，可见佩带吴钩在当时是一种显示少年英武风姿的时髦装束。

② 玉塞：指玉门关。

③ 关西：指函谷关。

Thinking of the Frontier

Li Yi (746~829)

The brocade belt with a sword round my waist,
Riding my horse I guard the autumn Yumen Pass.
Don't laugh at me as a general's son in the west,
I'd like to dedicate Liangzhou with my poetic ideas.

游子吟

孟郊 (751~814)

慈母手中线，游子身上衣。
临行密密缝，意恐迟迟归。
谁言寸草心，报得三春晖。

Wanderer's Song

Meng Jiao (751~814)

A lovely mother was sewing with a needle,
For a wanderer's clothes before farewell.
She did careful needlework for his travel,
She feared if her son will be late back home.
The young seedling grows one-inch strong,
Repaying mother's love three-spring long.

登科后

孟郊 (751~814)

昔日龌龊不足夸[1]，
今朝放荡思无涯。
春风得意马蹄疾，
一日看尽长安花。

【注释】

① 不足夸：不值得提起。

After Passing Imperial Examination

Meng Jiao (751~814)

Don’t praise how hard I studied more years ago,
I am unrestrained to think of the future I will endow.
My horse galloping through the proud spring breeze,
Within a day I look at all the Chang’an City’s flowers.

怨诗

孟郊 (751~814)

试妾与君泪，
两处滴池水。
看取芙蓉花，
今年为谁死！

Lovesickness

Meng Jiao (751~814)

Your tears and my tears from eyes into minds,
Our tears drop down into both of lotus ponds.
Let us see lotuses how pitifully to wither,
Who might be their love martyr this year!

早春呈水部张十八员外（其一）

韩愈 (768~824)

天街小雨润如酥，
草色遥看近却无。
最是一年春好处，
绝胜烟柳满皇都。

The Early Spring Dedicated to Zhang Ji

Han Yu (768~824)

The moist drizzle is dropping lightly from the heaven,
The grass afar look green but nearby no green seen.
The early spring is the best in changeable seasons,
The scene is prettier than royal willows in full green.

乌衣巷

刘禹锡 (772~842)

朱雀桥边野草花，
乌衣巷口夕阳斜。
旧时王谢堂前燕，
飞入寻常百姓家。

The Black Uniform Lane

Liu Yuxi (772~842)

Zhuque Bridge along with wild flowers in bloom,
The setting sun fell down Lane Black-Uniform.
Swallows once nestled at two top officials'*
mansions,
Nowadays they fly to the home of an ordinary
man.

* "Two top officials" refer to two Prime Ministers, namely, Wang Dao and Xie An in the Eastern Jin Dynasty (317~420).

朱雀橋邊野草花烏衣巷口
夕陽斜舊時王謝堂前燕
飛入尋常百姓家
仿大痴法寫劉禹錫句

竹枝词

刘禹锡 (772~842)

杨柳青青江水平，
闻郎岸上踏歌声。
东边日出西边雨，
道是无晴却有晴。

Bamboo Lyric

Liu Yuxi (772~842)

The peaceful river mirrors green willows young,
A girl is listening to her lover singing a folk song.
In the west it's rainy but the east is sunny,
The sky has no love but the day is lovely.

悯农诗

（二首）

李绅 (772~846)

一

锄禾日当午，汗滴禾下土。
谁知盘中餐，粒粒皆辛苦。

二

春种一粒粟，秋收万颗子。
四海无闲田，农夫犹饿死。

Commiserating Farmers

Li Shen (772~846)

One

The farmers are weeding at noon,
Sweating drops into the soil soon.
Who knows his own rice food on a tray,
Each grain came from the toiling day.

Two

Being sowed in spring is a millet grain,
Ten-thousand grains will be got in autumn.
Though there is no waste land with four seas,
Died of hunger, the farmers' harvest is useless.

赋得古原草送别

白居易 (772~846)

离离原上草，一岁一枯荣。
野火烧不尽，春风吹又生。
远芳侵古道，晴翠接荒城。
又送王孙去，萋萋满别情。

A Farewell Poem to the Old Meadow

Bai Juyi (772~846)

Grass is spreading over the old meadow,
Life or death will yearly come, yearly go.
The wild-fire can burn away the green,
Spring breeze will help it survive again.
The sweet green afar intrudes the old way,
The waste town meets it on a sunny day.
Seeing off my bosom friend again,
Still I feel strongly reluctant in pain.

花非花

白居易 (772~846)

花非花，雾非雾。
夜半来，天明去。
来如春梦几多时?
去似朝云无觅处。

It's Like a Flower But not a Flower*

Bai Juyi (772~846)

Like a flower but not a flower, like fog but not fog.
It's coming at midnight, and vanishing by daybreak.
Like a spring dream, how long will it last?
Like a morning cloud, where will it float?

* This poem was written by poet Bai Juyi to describe the prostitute singer's night lifeway.

琵琶行①（节选）

白居易(772~846)

千呼万唤始出来，
犹抱琵琶半遮面。
转轴拨弦三两声，
未成曲调先有情。

【注释】

① 本诗是白居易被贬官到江州时所作。作者借叙述琵琶女的高超技艺及凄凉身世，抒发自己政治上受打击遭贬斥的抑郁悲凄之情。

Quotation from *Pipa* Long Poem

Bai Juyi (772~846)

Long waiting later, she appeared with applause louder,
Half-face hidden, holding a lute in her lovely manner.
Shafts screwed and chords plucked twice or thrice gently,
As if she were foretelling lyric feelings before music play.

放言

（五首之三）

白居易 (772~846)

赠君一法决狐疑，
不用钻龟与祝蓍。
试玉要烧三日满，
辨材须待七年期。
周公[1]恐惧流言日，
王莽[2]谦恭未篡时。
向使当初身便死，
一生真伪复谁知？

Speak Frankly and Bluntly

Bai Juyi (772~846)

You need no suspicion I dedicate you a way,
Instead of what any fortune-teller would say.
Try to burn three days to test the pure jade,
Through seven years a talent would be proved.
Regent Duke Ji Dan's afraid of rumor or slander,
Wang Mang lost his modesty in usurped power.
If the regent top ruler passed away much early,
Who would know the truth with the false story?

【注释】

① 周公：即姬旦（约公元前 1100 年），周文王第四子，周武王弟，成王之叔。武王死，成王年幼，周公摄政，有人制造流言，诬蔑周公要篡位。周公于是避居于东，不问政事。后成王悔悟，迎回周公。在周代公为第一等爵位（公、侯、伯、子、男）。

② 王莽（公元前 45 年 ~ 公元 23 年），字巨君，中国历史上新朝的建立者，即新始祖，公元 8 年至公元 23 年在位。

长相思·汴水流

白居易 (772~846)

汴水流，泗水流，
流到瓜州古渡头。
吴山点点愁。

思悠悠，恨悠悠，
恨到归时方始休。
月明人倚楼。

Long Lovesickness · A Girl's Lyric

Bai Juyi (772~846)

The Bianshui creek in flow,
The Sishui creek in flow,
Toward Islet Guazhou, both flow,
Wu Peaks nod low.

My lovesickness is long,
And my hatred is strong.
I will go on in sorrow,
Till you return home.
Beneath the moonlight shadow,
I leant upon a balustrade pole.

长恨歌

白居易 (772~846)

汉皇①重色思倾国，
御宇多年求不得。
杨家有女初长成，
养在深闺人未识。

天生丽质难自弃，
一朝选在君王侧。
回眸一笑百媚生，
六宫粉黛无颜色。

【注释】

① 汉皇：原指汉武帝刘彻。这里指唐玄宗李隆基。

The Poem of Eternal Grief

Bai Juyi (772~846)

The lust emperor* thought of a nationwide
beautiful girl,
In his empire, spending years to seek for Beauty
but fail.
In Yang's** family, there's a girl growing mature,
Being secluded in deep boudoir no people know.

Her natural beauty could hardly keep her inside,
Once she was selected to the lust monarch's side.
Glancing back with a smile of one hundred times
charming,
She let six-palace imperial beauties no good-
looking.

* The lust emperor here actually refers to Emperor Li Longji (685~761), Tang Dynasty (618~907). His reign had lasted 43 years. In general, he was considered as a good emperor, and he promoted China to be powerful and prosperous and have the people living in good conditions. But later he began to corrupt, An-Shi Rebellion almost ruined Tang's power.

** Yang is a family name of Emperor Li Longji's beautiful concubine whose whole name is Yang Yuhuan (719~756). At the age of 27, she was registered as a concubine. On June 14, 756, she was forced to hang herself at Mawei Slope at the age of 38. Concubine Yang, Xi Shi, Wang Zhaojun, and Diao Chan are called "the four beauties of ancient China".

楊玉環
花露殿勸吸晨游紀貴妃
晚妝初罷鏡新浴乍披衣
宿酒醒還渴懷烟滴未晞
熟絲含碧荔涼抒汁红薇杯
裡珠圓乾閒前玉態肥乳香噴
欲亂畫痛咽猶微錦襪沾春露金
盤映曙暉華清宮外望餘影還芳菲
金閶馬駘製於滬上寓次

春寒赐浴华清池，
温泉水滑洗凝脂。
侍儿扶起娇无力，
始是新承恩泽时。

云鬓花颜金步摇，
芙蓉帐暖度春宵。
春宵苦短日高起，
从此君王不早朝。

承欢侍宴无闲暇，
春从春游夜专夜。
后宫佳丽三千人，
三千宠爱在一身。

金屋妆成娇侍夜，
玉楼宴罢醉和春。
姊妹弟兄皆列土，
可怜光彩生门户。

She's granted to bathe in Huaqing-Pool in cold
spring,
Hot spring water smoothly washed her pretty fatty
skin.
The maid propped up for she was too frail,
She started to sense thanks-giving the royal.

Her phoenix coronet with a hairpin Gold Pendant,
She spent spring night to shelter in warm lotus
tent.
Spring night was too short to stop daybreak,
The Emperor could not go for timely work.

Her joy was from monarch's joy to share dinner
busily,
Spring outing's by day with pleasure at night
mutually.
In back palace, there were three thousand beauties
totally,
Only one out of three thousand belonged to most
lovely.

In her gold chamber she put on makeup, a maid
served,
After Jade Pavilion's banquet, she was a bit
inebriated.
Her sisters and brothers were bestowed of fief and
rank,
Her family turned glorious and fortunate with
good luck.

遂令天下父母心， 不重生男重生女。 骊宫高处入青云， 仙乐风飘处处闻。	Then all the world parents changed of thinking way, They all wanted to give a birth of girl instead of boy. The imperial Li-Palace stood up to the cloud sky, Fairy beauties' music heard of breeze passing by.
缓歌慢舞凝丝竹， 尽日君王看不足。 渔阳鼙鼓动地来， 惊破霓裳羽衣曲。	Music instruments helped singing and dancing tardily, The monarch turned greedy to appreciate all the day. The warring drum was beaten fast in City Yuyang, Surprisingly to calm down Rainbow-Plumage song.
九重城阙烟尘生， 千乘万骑西南行。 翠华摇摇行复止， 西出都门百余里。	The war fire over capital city with nine gates, To flee west-southward were chariots and knights. The banners flutter, guard army moving off or on, Away from the west gate they fled one hundred miles long.
六军不发无奈何， 宛转蛾眉马前死。 花钿委地无人收， 翠翘金雀玉搔头。	The Six-Army didn't move on, Emperor was helpless, His concubine was forced to hang herself before horses. Flowery ornaments' out of her hair, no one to collect, Either Jade-feather, Golden-bird or Ruby-pendant.

君王掩面救不得，
回看血泪相和流。
黄埃散漫风萧索，
云栈萦纡登剑阁。

峨嵋山下少人行，
旌旗无光日色薄。
蜀江水碧蜀山青，
圣主朝朝暮暮情。

行宫见月伤心色，
夜雨闻铃肠断声。
天旋地转回龙驭，
到此踌躇不能去。

马嵬坡下泥土中，
不见玉颜空死处。
君臣相顾尽沾衣，
东望都门信马归。

The monarch covered his face with no way to rescue,
Just looking back to her blood and tears, also tearful.
The yellow dust scattering, the wind seemed to weep,
Cloud-cliff road zigzagged to the Sword-Pass Stop.

Few people had often passed by the Emei Mountain,
The imperial banners seemed dim with the faint sun.
Shu's rivers looked blue, mountains in dark green,
Day and night the monarch's lovesick time and again.

At dwelling palace he looked up at the moon in pain,
He was heart-broken while he was listening to the rain.
The empire turned upside down, his Dragon Chariot back,
Still he stopped at Mawei Slope to hesitate for going back.

Emperor's concubine buried in Mawei Slope eternally,
Her jade-like face could no longer be seen anyway.
Emperor met ministers, tears falling into his robe,
Looking at East Gate, they had horses to follow.

归来池苑皆依旧，
太液芙蓉未央柳。
芙蓉如面柳如眉，
对此如何不泪垂！

春风桃李花开日，
秋雨梧桐叶落时。
西宫南内多秋草，
落叶满阶红不扫。

梨园子弟白发新，
椒房阿监青娥老。
夕殿萤飞思悄然，
孤灯挑尽未成眠。

迟迟钟鼓初长夜，
耿耿星河欲曙天。
鸳鸯瓦冷霜华重，
翡翠衾寒谁与共？

Back home, pool or garden seen as the original,
The Taiye Lake still mirrored hibiscus or willow.
Hibiscus meant her face or eyebrows as weeping willow,
Watching such scenery, he couldn't help being tearful.

Spring breeze brought peach and plum to bloom,
Autumn rain had phoenix trees' leaves fall in gloom.
In West or South-Inner Palace grew more autumn grass,
The stone steps are full of withered leaves or faded flowers.

The newly white-haired drama troupe disciples looked fresh,
The old-looking eunuchs and maids remained in Jiao Palace.
At dusk the palace fireflies flying made him silently lovesick,
At night he failed to sleep, just stirring up his lamp-wick.

The delaying Bell and Drum waited for an initial long night,
The luminous stars and Milky Way yearned for dawn light.
Cold flowery frost covered lovebird-like flawless tiles,
Who could come in to share the cool emerald quilts?

悠悠生死别经年，
魂魄不曾来入梦。
临邛道士鸿都客，
能以精诚致魂魄。

为感君王辗转思，
遂教方士殷勤觅。
排空驭气奔如电，
升天入地求之遍。

上穷碧落下黄泉，
两处茫茫皆不见。
忽闻海上有仙山，
山在虚无缥缈间。

楼阁玲珑五云起，
其中绰约多仙子。
中有一人字太真，
雪肤花貌参差是。

The alive parted the dead with an eternal farewell,
The monarch had no longer dreamed of her soul.
Linqiong Taoist invited as a magician to serve in the capital,
He helped the emperor show loyalty toward the Beautiful.

Monarch's lovesick toss and turn stirred up the magician,
Then being ordered to seek for her soul time and again.
Flying up to the vast sky as fast as lightning thunder,
From the heaven to the earth, Taoist magic everywhere.

Searching from the above sky into her netherworld below,
As a result, failed, there was no concubine soul's shadow.
Abruptly fairyland was told to emerge on the ocean,
That stood up like a mirage from Penglai-Pavilion.

The colorful clouds hovered pavilions and towers tinkling,
Many fairy beauties looked more attractively charming.
One of whom was meaningfully named Everlasttruly,
Her skin was in snow-white, her lovely face's flowery.

金阙西厢叩玉扃，
转教小玉报双成。
闻道汉家天子使，
九华帐里梦魂惊。

揽衣推枕起徘徊，
珠箔银屏迤逦开。
云鬓半偏新睡觉，
花冠不整下堂来。

风吹仙袂飘飖举，
犹似霓裳羽衣舞。
玉容寂寞泪阑干，
梨花一枝春带雨。

含情凝睇谢君王，
一别音容两渺茫。
昭阳殿里恩爱绝，
蓬莱宫中日月长。

Gold-palace west chamber's door was lightly
knocked,
Petty-Jade was told to report to Double-Maturely
maid.
Everlasttruly heard of a Han-dynasty's envoy
being to come,
Within flowery tent she was surprised to break out
her dream.

Putting on clothes to push pillow aside, uneasy to
wander,
She rolled up her pearl curtain and screen in silver
color.
Just she woke up, her temples' hairs in semi-disorder,
Her coronet bun inclined aside when she left the door.

The wind was blowing fairy sleeves to float up freely,
She was dancing a Rainbow-Plumage-Dance
originally.
Alone her tears dropped on the railing,
As a pear twig was full of rain in spring.

Her eyes full of tender feelings to thank for her
monarch,
Once one passed away, the two would be deeply
lovesick.
The Brilliant-Palace lost all of the conjugal love
light,
The Penglai Palace locked by the sunshine and
moonlight.

回头下望人寰处，
不见长安见尘雾。
惟将旧物表深情，
钿合金钗寄将去。

钗留一股合一扇，
钗擘黄金合分钿。
但教心似金钿坚，
天上人间会相见。

临别殷勤重寄词，
词中有誓两心知。
七月七日长生殿，
夜半无人私语时。

在天愿作比翼鸟，
在地愿为连理枝。
天长地久有时尽，
此恨绵绵无绝期。

Looking back to watch the human world, small or big,
No Capital City Chang'an was seen, just dust or fog.
Only her original ornament used to show her deeply
loyalty,
She would send her gold hairpin with her good
memory.

The jewelry box or pair of hairpins separated into
two evenly,
Half of ornaments distributed to each other as
good memory.
She wished two hearts be like pair of gold ornament,
The love couple in paradise would eventually reunite.

At parting time, she took seriously sending
lovesick words,
That two hearts' were tacit understanding as soul-
mate.
In the Long-Life Palace on the romantic Double
Seventh Day,
She wrote an oath at midnight when no one had a
word to say.

Be a pair of lovebirds, wing to wing, flying in the
skyline end,
Be a pair of sprigs, side by side, growing in the
same land.
The endless heaven or earth may be inevitably
changeable,
The unending lovesick grief or sorrow will be
eternally stable.

题都城南庄

崔护 (772~846)

去年今日此门中，
人面桃花相映红。
人面不知何处去，
桃花依旧笑春风。

Inscription to the Urban Suburb South Village

Cui Hu (772~846)

This day last year a girl was leaning at the gate,
Her shy-flushed face and the peach blossom were the same.
The shy-flushed girl did not know where to go today,
Peach blossoms still smile at spring breeze as that day.

江雪

柳宗元 (773~819)

千山鸟飞绝，
万径人踪灭。
孤舟蓑笠翁，
独钓寒江雪。

The River in Snowing

Liu Zongyuan (773~819)

Over mountains no birds fly high or low,
Along every road no people were on the go.
Alone an old fisher wore a straw raincoat,
He was fishing on his snowing-river boat.

千山鳥飛絶萬徑人蹤滅
孤舟蓑笠翁獨釣寒江雪
乙丑秋九月寫柳宗元句
邛池漁父馬駘作于滬上

离思
（五首之四）

元稹 (779~831)

曾经沧海难为水，
除却巫山不是云。
取次花丛懒回顾，
半缘修道半缘君。

Lovesick Farewell

Yuan Zhen (779~831)

Not any water could attract me, while experiencing
the deep sea.
It's worth seeing no cloud again, but the pretty
fairy Wu Mountain.
I was lazy to look back any flowers,
I love you as I believed in a religion.

剑客

贾岛 (779~843)

十年磨一剑，
霜刃[①]未曾试。
今日把示君，
谁有不平事？

A Chivalrous Swordsman

Jia Dao (779~843)

Ten years were spent in sharpening my sword,
Its frosty-white blade has never been tested.
I would like to show you the sword today,
Have you something too unjust to say?

【注释】

① 霜刃：形容剑刃十分锋利。

金缕衣

作者不详

劝君莫惜金缕衣，
劝君惜取少年时。
花开堪折直须[①]折，
莫待无花空折枝。

The Golden Dress

Anonymous

Advise you not to treasure your golden dress,
Advise you to treasure your golden youth times.
Pick a flower in time when it grows in full bloom,
Don’t pick a flowerless branch with no blossom.

【注释】

① 直须：不要犹豫。

宫词
（其一）

张祜 (792~854)

故国三千里，
深宫二十年。
一声何满子[①]，
双泪落君前。

【注释】

① 何满子：唐教坊曲名。本为唐玄宗时著名歌者，据说她因故得罪了皇帝，被推出就刑。就刑前她张口高歌，曲调悲愤，使“苍天白日黯然失色”。结果皇帝闻之，终因惜其技艺难得而降旨缓刑。因为何满子出色的技艺，大诗人元稹、白居易、杜牧等都相继为之赋诗，其中以张祜的《何满子》宫词，最为感人。

Palace Lyrics

Zhang Hu (792~854)

Leaving homeland three thousand miles far away,
In deep palace, she sang twenty years, day by day.
Hemanzi was sung by me as a sorrowful lyric,
Her eyes full of tears, facing her monarch.

泊秦淮

杜牧 (803~852)

烟笼寒水月笼沙，
夜泊秦淮近酒家。
商女[①]不知亡国恨，
隔江犹唱后庭花[②]。

Mooring at Qinhuai Moat

Du Mu (803~852)

The haze covered the cold river beach in the moonlight,
The boats were moored at night tavern to the riverside.
Dancing girls had no idea of state-conquered doom,
Ashore still sing a song, the *Backyard Flowers Bloom*.

【注释】

① 商女：以卖唱为生的歌女。

② 后庭花：指《玉树后庭花》。

江南春

杜牧 (803~852)

千里莺啼绿映红，
水村山郭酒旗风。
南朝四百八十寺，
多少楼台烟雨中？

Spring in the South Riverside

Du Mu (803~852)

The remote-flying orioles sing over the vast red dotting green,
The wind flutters Inn Banners through the river and mountain.
The South-Dynasty has built four-hundred and eighty temples,
How many Buddhist pavilions and towers beaten by the rain?

过华清宫

杜牧 (803~852)

长安回望绣成堆，
山顶千门次第开。
一骑红尘妃子笑，
无人知是荔枝来。

Passing Huaqing Palace

Du Mu (803~852)

Looking back Capital City's embroidered-like mountain,
The palace with consecutive gates is orderly open.
The concubine smiled at a galloping knight in dust-flow,
That her favorite fruit litchi at arrival, no people know.

赤壁

杜牧 (803~852)

折戟沉沙铁未销，
自将磨洗认前朝。
东风不与周郎便，
铜雀春深锁二乔。

The Red-Cliff

Du Mu (803~852)

The broken halberd was sunk into the river
bottom,
That was unearthed to recognize original kingdom.
Without the East Wind to help Zhou Yu to win,
Their two-beauties would be locked in Tongque
Pavilion.

二喬
國色人間少喬家竟得雙書傳
黃石筍觀向碧紗窗
馬駘畫

山行

杜牧 (803~852)

远上寒山石径斜，
白云生处有人家。
停车坐爱枫林晚，
霜叶红于二月花。

Walking in the Mountains

Du Mu (803~852)

Climbing the cold hill afar on a rocky way,
I saw white clouds rising from the family.
I stopped my cart to look at the late maple,
Whose leaves redder than flowers in vernal.

遠上寒山石徑斜白雲深處
有人家停車坐愛楓林晚
霜葉紅於二月花
馬駘寫杜牧句於滬上

陇西行①

陈陶 (812~885)

誓扫匈奴不顾身，
五千貂锦丧胡尘。
可怜无定河边骨，
犹是春闺梦里人。

The West-Frontier Verse*

Chen Tao (812~885)

Fear no sacrifice to swear sweeping the Huns was
our army,
Five thousand of soldiers in mink-uniform fought
to death bravely.
It was a pity the martyrs' bones buried along the
riverside,
Each of which is still dreamed by his young
maiden in mind.

【注释】

① 行：乐府古诗中的一种体裁。《陇西行》为古代歌曲名，是乐府《相和歌·瑟调曲》旧题，内容写边塞战争。

* Usually, the title was used as an ancient music title in the Tang Dynasty (618~907).

无题二首

（其一）

李商隐 (813~858)

昨夜星辰昨夜风，
画楼西畔桂堂东。
身无彩凤双飞翼，
心有灵犀一点通①。

隔座送钩②春酒暖，
分曹射覆③蜡灯红。
嗟余听鼓应官去，
走马兰台类转蓬。

【注释】

① 心有灵犀一点通：比喻人与人心灵上易于沟通，容易达成共识或默契。

② 送钩：也称藏钩。古代腊日的一种游戏，把钩或指环等物互相传送后，藏于一人手中，令人猜。

③ 射覆：在覆器下放着东西令人猜。分曹、射覆未必是实指，只是借题发挥。

An Untitled Poem

Li Shangyin (813~858)

Last night stars were bright, last night the wind on blow,
A banquet held from the chamber west to the east hall.
Without phoenix double wings, I cannot fly to you,
Two minds think alike to let love road easily go.

The ring-hidden-games loser had to drink of alcohol,
Under candle light two groups tried to guess " yes or no".
Regretfully, timekeeping-drum let me work in official hall,
I had to run to my official department like a speeding ball.

无题

李商隐 (813~858)

相见时难别亦难，
东风无力百花残。
春蚕到死丝方尽，
蜡炬成灰泪始干。

晓镜但愁云鬓改，
夜吟应觉月光寒。
蓬山①此去无多路，
青鸟②殷勤为探看。

An Untitled Poem

Li Shangyin (813~858)

It's difficult to meet you again, also difficult to farewell,
The east wind seemed too weak to keep flowers well.
Before dying spring silkworms must spin silks at all,
Until burning candles turned ashes, tears always flow.

The mirror reflects my temples' hair grey with sorrow,
At night reading aloud, I felt the moonlight was cold.
To Penglai fairyland we had hardly have roads to go,
Yet the hospitality bird might explore it to show you.

【注释】

① 蓬山：蓬莱山，传说为海上仙山。

② 青鸟：神话中为西王母传递音讯的信使。

夜雨寄北

李商隐 (813~858)

君问归期未有期，
巴山[1]夜雨涨秋池。
何当共剪西窗烛，
却话[2]巴山夜雨时。

A Letter to My Love at Rainy Night

Li Shangyin (813~858)

I can hardly foretell when to enjoy our reunion,
To see the Autumn Pond full with a night rain.
We cannot shear up a candle wick at the west window,
Until I can tell you night rain falls on Ba Mountain.

【注释】

① 巴山：重庆古代属巴国。此处泛指重庆一带的山。

② 却话：重头谈起。

乐游原

李商隐 (813~858)

向晚[①]意不适，
驱车登古原[②]。
夕阳无限好，
只是近[③]黄昏。

【注释】

① 向晚：傍晚。
② 古原：指乐游原。
③ 近：快要。

Plain of Imperial Tombs

Li Shangyin (813~858)

At evening, my heart was full of gloom,
I drove my cart to wheel along the ancient tomb.
The setting sun looks unlimitedly good-looking,
Just soon it's to be buried by the night-coming.

向晚意不適驅車登古原
夕陽無限好只是近黃昏
乙丑秋馬駘寫李商隱句

题菊花

黄巢 (820?~884)

飒飒西风满院栽，
蕊寒香冷蝶难来。
他年我若为青帝[①]，
报与桃花一处开。

Inscription to Chrysanthemum

Huang Chao (820?~884)

The whole yard was full of west wind soughing in
blow,
The yellow chrysanthemum planted vigorously to
grow.
All the pistils were fragrant but cold,
So it's difficult for butterflies to hold.
If I become the emperor of spring in the future,
All the peaches should be bloom with you together.

【注释】

① 青帝：司春之神。

不第①后赋菊

黄巢 (820?~884)

待得秋来九月八，
我花开后百花杀②。
冲天香阵透长安，
满城尽带黄金甲。

Ode to Chrysanthemum after Failure of Imperial Examination

Huang Chao (820?~884)

Before the autumn coming on September-Eighth day,
Chrysanthemum blooming, hundreds of flowers faded away.
Floating over Capital Chang'an is in fragrant smell,
The city is full of gold-armored-like flowers in yellow.

【注释】

① 不第：科举落第。

② 杀：草木枯萎。

送人游吴

杜荀鹤 (846~904)

君到姑苏见，人家尽枕河。
古宫闲地少，水巷小桥多。

夜市卖菱藕，春船载绮罗。
遥知未眠月，乡思在渔歌。

Travels in Gusu with My Pal

Du Xunhe (846~904)

Visiting Gusu City, what do you know?
The citizens used to take creek as pillow.
The imperial palace has less free places,
The narrow lane has more little bridges.

At night markets lotus seeds are on sale,
The boat carries silk products in vernal.
I know the remote moon lying sleepless,
A fishing song had me in homesickness.

题红叶

唐代僖宗年间宫女（佚名）

流水何太急，
深宫尽日闲。
殷勤谢红叶，
好去到人间。

Lyric Inscription on a Leaf

Palace Maid (Anonymous)

Why the water is so fast to flow?
In the deep palace it runs slow.
Let me thank the red leaf hospitably,
For sending my lyric to the humanity.

春怨

金昌绪 (唐代诗人，生卒年不详)

打起黄莺儿，
莫教枝上啼。
啼时惊妾梦，
不得到辽西。

Plaint in Spring

Jin Changxu (birth and death unknown)

I throw a stone at an oriole in yellow,
In order to stop its singing in the willow.
For the bird's noises have broken my dream,
Of Liaoxi where my army lover is to go home.

采桑子[①]

（版本一）

花蕊夫人[②](883~926)

初离蜀道心将碎，
离恨绵绵，
春日如年，
马上时时闻杜鹃。

三千宫女皆花貌，
共斗婵娟，
髻学朝天，
今日谁知是谶言[③]。

To the Melody of Picking-Mulberry

(Version A)

Madam Huarui (883~926)

Leaving my native road, my heart was broken,
With parting lingering pain,
A spring day was like a year-season,
On horseback I heard of cuckoo time and again.

All the three thousand maids looked prettier,
As if the moon and Big Dipper glitter,
They combed in high-bun hair,
Who knows that's an augury of fortune-teller.

【注释】

① 这首《采桑子》当时并没有写完，下阕为后人所续，还有人这样续写讽刺花蕊夫人："三千宫女如花面，妾最婵娟，此去朝天，只恐君王宠爱偏。"

② 花蕊夫人：此处指后蜀主孟昶的费贵妃，历史上除了费贵妃，还有前蜀主王建淑妃徐氏和南唐李煜的宫人被誉为花蕊夫人。

③ 谶（chèn）言：指古代占卜，预测吉凶。

采桑子
（版本二）

花蕊夫人 (883~926)

初离蜀道心将碎，
离恨绵绵，
春日如年，
马上时时闻杜鹃。

三千宫女如花面，
妾最婵娟，
此去朝天，
只恐君王宠爱偏。

To the Melody of Picking-Mulberry
(Version B)

Madam Huarui (883~926)

Leaving my native road, my heart was broken,
With parting lingering pain,
A spring day was like a year-season,
On horseback I heard of cuckoo time and again.

Three thousand maids looked flowery.
I was the best like the moon only,
I ’d like to see the heaven ruler,
Only worried I would lose the emperor’s favor.

述国亡诗

花蕊夫人 (883~926)

君王城上竖降旗，
妾在深宫那得知。
十四万人齐解甲，
宁无一个是男儿。

An Imperial Concubine's Poem

Madam Huarui (883~926)

The emperor's surrender flag hung over the city,
As an imperial concubine, I did not know his pity.
140,000 soldiers cast off the armor and weapon,
No one of them was as brave as a great true man.

咏初日

赵匡胤 (927~976)

欲出未出光辣达，
千山万山如火发。
须臾走向天上来，
逐却残星赶却月。

Ode to the Sun

Zhao Kuangyin (927~976)

The morning sun is shyly rising up gradually,
Myriad mountains seem to be burning wildly.
In a moment it is like going to the sky soon,
All the residual stars are swept with the moon.

虞美人

李煜[①] (937~978)

春花秋月何时了？
往事知多少。
小楼昨夜又东风，
故国不堪回首月明中。

雕栏玉砌应犹在，
只是朱颜改。
问君能有几多愁？
恰似一江春水向东流。

Beautiful Lady Yu

Li Yu (937~978)

When will the autumn moon stop rising or falling?
When will spring flowers stop blooming or fading?
How many past events? Who knows?
The east wind still blew my chamber last night,
I reluctantly recalled my native land in the
moonlight.

Standing still is my palace jade-like railing of
marble,
Yet my ruddy face looked changeable.
How much about your great sorrow?
That's just like a spring river to flow.

【注释】

① 李煜：南唐最后一位国君，人称李后主。南唐是五代十国的十国之一，定都金陵，历时39年，有先主李昪、中主李璟和后主李煜三位帝王。南唐一朝，最盛时幅员35州。南唐三世在五代乱世中“比年丰稔，兵食有余”，是中国历史上重要的政权之一。

相见欢

李煜 (937~978)

无言独上西楼，
月如钩，
寂寞梧桐深院锁清秋。
剪不断，
理还乱，
是离愁，
别是一番滋味在心头。

Joyful Reunion

Li Yu (937~978)

Upstairs voicelessly I'd like to go,
The moon is like a bow,
The deep courtyard is to hold,
Lonely parasol tree to lock autumn cold.
It is impossible to cut off my sorrow,
I comb up but fail,
No way to cancel the parting sorrow,
In my heart it's a special farewell.

浪淘沙令

李煜 (937~978)

帘外雨潺潺，
春意阑珊。
罗衾不耐五更寒。
梦里不知身是客，
一晌贪欢。

独自莫凭栏，
无限江山，
别时容易见时难。
流水落花春去也，
天上人间。

Billows Cleaning out Sands

Li Yu (937~978)

It's drizzling outside my curtain,
Spring in the air is waning again.
The silk quilt couldn't keep me night warm.
I don't know I'm a captive bird in my dream,
I try to have it as happy as home.

Don't be lonely to lean upon balustrade,
Looking over the boundless vast land,
That's easy lost but hard got.
With the running water, fallen flowers float,
  spring has disappeared.
The paradise is no longer my human world.

雨霖铃

柳永 (987~1053)

寒蝉凄切，
对长亭晚，
骤雨初歇。
都门帐饮无绪，
方留恋处，
兰舟催发。
执手相看泪眼，
竟无语凝噎。
念去去，千里烟波，
暮霭沉沉楚天阔。

多情自古伤离别，
更那堪，
冷落清秋节！
今宵酒醒何处？
杨柳岸，
晓风残月。
此去经年，
应是良辰好景虚设。
便纵有千种风情，
更与何人说！

Rain Click Bell

Liu Yong (987~1053)

The cold cicada is sadly whining,
Against the distant bower in the evening,
A sudden downpour has a rest.
I'm in the tent outside the city gate,
I'm drinking to feel gloomy in disorder.
Reluctant to be apart from each other,
I watch the boat awaiting me to sail afar.
Mutually holding hands to see eyes tearful,
Both say nothing but too much sorrow.
Thinking of one thousand mile distance misty
riverside,
I imagined the dusk haze to be deep, and the sky
wide.

Farewell full of lovesickness since the ancient
time,
Especially it's on the autumn festival under
moonlight.
Where I would be when I awoke from wine
tonight?
It's the poplar-willow-shore of the riverside,
Where the breeze blew and the crescent bright.
My long trip would fail to enjoy the scenic sight.
Even if the romantic events were myriad in mind,
No one could understand why I sigh.

苏幕遮

范仲淹 (989~1052)

碧云天，
黄叶地。
秋色连波，
波上寒烟翠。
山映斜阳天接水，
芳草无情，
更在斜阳外。

黯乡魂，
追旅思。
夜夜除非，
好梦留人睡。
明月楼高休独倚，
酒入愁肠，
化作相思泪。

Sumuzhe Pretty Apparel

Fan Zhongyan (989~1052)

It is a bluish cloudy sky,
The leaves cover the ground like yellow dye.
The autumn scenery seems to be in flow,
The verdant fog is cold like the white billow.
Over hills the setting-sun lying under the sky,
The fragrant grass has no love sense as human
mind,
Spreading outside is the setting-sun light.

I am melancholy to be homesick of my traveling
memories to seek.
Every night only my deep hearty bottom,
That could help me enter a good dream.
My mansion is so high, the bright moon could not
lean upon it to shine.
My heart was broken with the wine,
To turn my lovesick tears dropping in mind.

渔家傲

范仲淹 (989~1052)

塞下秋来风景异，
衡阳雁去无留意。
四面边声连角起。
千嶂里，
长烟落日孤城闭。

浊酒一杯家万里，
燕然未勒归无计。
羌管悠悠霜满地。
人不寐，
将军白发征夫泪。

Fisherman Pride

Fan Zhongyan (989~1052)

The coming autumn brought different scenery to
the frontier army,
The wild geese left for flying to Hengyang, no
longer to stay.
Everywhere in the border region, warring horns
call on consecutively.
Over thousands of peaks,
Signal-smoke camouflaging the setting sun, the
lonely city blocks.

One cup of the bitter wine is associated with the
ten thousand mile home back again,
However, there's no reason to return, for no triumph
inscription carved upon the Yanran Mountain.
The *Qiang* flute is floating leisurely.
The army men are unable to be sleepy.
Fighters shedding tears, Generals' hairs turn grey.

剔银灯[①]

与欧阳公[②]席上分题

范仲淹 (989~1052)

昨夜因看蜀志，
笑曹操、孙权、刘备。
用尽机关，
徒劳心力，
只得三分天地。
屈指细寻思，
争如共、
刘伶[③]一醉。

Up Lifting Silver Lantern*

Fan Zhongyan (989~1052)

Reading Shu-chronicles till midnight, yesterday,
I laughed at Three Kingdoms' Cao Cao, Sun Quan
and Liu Bei.
Plotting and scheming too much in tricky way,
Working hard but in vain,
Just winning as one-third China as a gain.
Counting on their fingers carefully,
The Three Kingdoms shared each share willingly
by intrigues different from scholar Liu Ling's
way.

【注释】

① 词牌名。宋词流行时其词牌多得惊人，仅由三个字为词牌的、首字为十笔画的就有八十多个，《剔银灯》是其中之一。

② 欧阳公：指欧阳修。

③ 刘伶、阮籍、嵇康、山涛、阮咸、向秀、王戎是魏末晋初的七位名士。其中最为著名的酒徒是刘伶。刘伶自谓："天生刘伶，以酒为名，一饮一斛，五斗解酲。"

* *Up Lifting Silver Lantern* is a music title being popular as a tune or melody for singing different lyric poems in the Song Dynasty (960~1279).

人世都无百岁。
少痴騃[4]、
老成尪悴[5]。
只有中间，些子少年，
忍把浮名牵系。
一品与千金，
问白发、
如何回避。

Nobody's longevity was one-hundred-year long.
Idiotic or silly when the child was early young,
Turning aged, one would not be strong.
It's only the middle-aged guy,
That has an empty glory to try,
As no one is not greedy to occupy both a highest position and a beautiful concubine.
One's gray hair could tell why,
No way to stop your hair turning white.

④ 騃（ái）：呆傻。
⑤ 尪（wāng）悴：衰老羸弱的样子。

江上渔者

范仲淹 (989~1052)

江上往来人，
但爱鲈鱼美。
君看一叶舟，
出没风波里。

River Fisherman

Fan Zhongyan (989~1052)

Along the riverside people come and go,
Perch's delicious no one does not know.
But do you see a leaf-like fishing boat,
Rolling up and down the windy billow.

过苏州

苏舜钦[1] (1008~1048)

东出蟠门[2]刮眼明，
萧萧疏雨更阴晴。
绿杨白鹭俱自得，
近水远山皆有情。
万物盛衰天意在，
一身羁苦俗人轻。
无穷好景无缘住，
旅棹[3]区区暮亦行。

Passing Suzhou

Su Shunqin (1008~1048)

Outside the town's gate, my eyes seem bright,
Drizzling later, it may be cloudy or a fine day.
Over green poplars, white cranes fly in my sight,
An affectionate river flows along the far hill away.
Predestined is your value being low or high,
Officials' paces are heavy, folks are light.
No chance to stay in such an endless scenic site,
The passenger ship is still hurrying away at twilight.

【注释】

① 苏舜钦：北宋诗人，曾任大理评事，被范仲淹推荐为集贤校理、监进奏院。宋仁宗庆历四年（1044），因"稍侵权贵"，革职为民。退居苏州，买水石，筑沧浪亭。

② 蟠门：又作盘门，苏州城的西南门。

③ 旅棹（zhào）：客船。

元日

王安石 (1021~1086)

爆竹声中一岁除，
春风送暖入屠苏①。
千门万户曈曈②日，
总把新桃换旧符。

On the First Day of Chinese New Year

Wang Anshi (1021~1086)

With the sound of firecrackers, the New Year is
coming, the Old is going out,
Spring breeze has home-made wine warm.
All families enjoy sunshine outside the room,
Let newly-painted peach-board lucky charm
replaces the old to protect home.

【注释】

① 屠苏：古代用屠苏草泡制的一种酒。

② 曈曈（tóng tóng）：初升的太阳照亮大地时的景色。

春夜

王安石 (1021~1086)

金炉香烬漏① 声残，
翦翦② 轻风阵阵寒。
春色恼人眠不得，
月移花影上栏干。

【注释】

① 漏：指"铜壶滴漏"，即漏壶，又称刻漏或漏刻，是中国古代自动化计时（测量时间）装置。

② 翦翦（jiǎn jiǎn）：形容风轻且有点寒意。

Spring Night

Wang Anshi (1021~1086)

Gold censer full of embers, the Pot-Timer* drops weakly,
The gently gentle breeze is blowing coldly and coldly.
I'm sleepless for spring scenery's lured and annoyed,
The moon has moved flowers' shadow on balustrade.

* The Pot-Timer is a kind of device to measure time in ancient times.

泊船瓜洲

王安石 (1021~1086)

京口瓜洲一水间，
钟山只隔数重山。
春风又绿江南岸，
明月何时照我还？

Mooring at Guazhou Isle

Wang Anshi (1021~1086)

The river goes around Guazhou Isle beside
Jingkou,
Passing a few hills, I will arrive at my Zhongshan
goal.
The spring breeze has had the south riverside green,
When will the bright moon see me going back
again?

秋月

程颢 (1032~1085)

清溪流过碧山头，
空水澄鲜一色秋。
隔断红尘三十里，
白云红叶两悠悠。

The Autumn Moon

Cheng Hao (1032~1085)

The clean creek goes around the green mountain,
Under the sky the water mirrors a fresh autumn.
Far away from the human world for thirty miles,
The white clouds leisurely look at the red maples.

惠崇春江晚景（其一）

苏轼 (1037~1101)

竹外桃花三两枝，
春江水暖鸭先知。
蒌蒿满地芦芽短，
正是河豚欲上时。

An Inscription on the Painting of Spring-River Scenery

Su Shi (1037~1101)

Outside bamboos two or three peach twigs bloom,
The ducks can foretell the spring river to be warm.
The asparagus shoots grow short, potherbs full in
green,
It is exactly time that returning puffer fish are in
season.

江城子
乙卯正月二十日夜记梦

苏轼 (1037~1101)

十年生死两茫茫，
不思量，自难忘。
千里孤坟，无处话凄凉。
纵使相逢应不识，
尘满面，鬓如霜。

夜来幽梦忽还乡，
小轩窗，正梳妆。
相顾无言，惟有泪千行。
料得年年肠断处，
明月夜，短松冈。

The Riverside City

Su Shi (1037~1101)

Passing away, you left me alone ten years long,
Self-thinking of you, my lovesickness was strong.
Your tomb's far, far away,
How I could tell you my loneliness day by day.
You might not recognize me even if I met you
anew,
My face's dusty, and my hair gray.

At night suddenly I dreamed of returning home,
Facing your dressing table to comb,
Silently we looked at each other, tears flew.
Year in year out, I am too sad with your tomb,
At moonlight night, short pines accompany your
"room".

念奴娇
赤壁怀古

苏轼 (1037~1101)

大江东去，浪淘尽，
千古风流人物。
故垒西边，人道是：
三国周郎赤壁。
乱石穿空，惊涛拍岸，
卷起千堆雪。
江山如画，
一时多少豪杰。

A Pretty Dancing Girl
Meditating on the Heroic Story of the Red Cliff

Su Shi (1037~1101)

Rolling eastward is the Great River,
Cleaning heroes out one after another,
Never stop from year to year.
Near an old rampart's west side,
Called Marshal Zhou's Red-Cliff,
That stood up since the Three Kingdoms time.
The disordered crags jump up to the sky,
While frightened billows whipping the riverside,
Wave upon wave, in snowy white.
Such a land with the picture-like sight,
That moved myriad heroes to fight.

遥想公瑾当年，
小乔初嫁了，雄姿英发。
羽扇纶巾，谈笑间，
樯橹灰飞烟灭。
故国神游，多情应笑我，
早生华发。
人生如梦，
一樽还酹江月。

I recalled what happened to Marshal Zhou,
That married Xiaoqiao, a beautiful girl.
How heroic he looked in style!
The military genius leisurely waved his feather fan,
Wearing his hat with black silk ribbon,
Talking and laughing at the foes' warships burnt
into dust just in a moment.
I might be laughed at my emotional memories of
the past,
For my hairs should not turn grey so fast.
That life is like a dream to be broken soon,
Empty a cup of wine to worship the river and
moon.

望湖楼醉书①

（其一）

苏轼 (1037~1101)

黑云翻墨②未遮山，
白雨跳珠乱入船。
卷地风来忽吹散，
望湖楼下水如天。

My Tipsy Writing to the Lake-Watchtower

Su Shi (1037~1101)

Rolling up and down, black clouds covered no mountain,
Jumping up and down the boat is a lingering pure rain.
Suddenly the ground-rolling wind is to drive the rain away,
The lake-watchtower below looks like a human Milky Way.

【注释】

① 这是苏轼谪居杭州期间所创作的一组七言绝句，共五首。本诗是第一首。“望湖楼”位于杭州西湖湖畔，又叫看经楼。

② 翻墨：打翻的黑墨水，形容云层很黑。

饮湖上初晴后雨

苏轼 (1037~1101)

水光潋滟晴方好，
山色空蒙雨亦奇。
欲把西湖比西子，
淡妆浓抹总相宜。

Drinking on the West Lake at First Sunny, Later Rainy

Su Shi (1037~1101)

Just now sunny, wavy water glittering brilliantly,
The odd rain made all the hills misty and empty.
Compared between the West Lake and the Beauty,
It looks so pretty regardless of makeup light or
heavy.

水调歌头

苏轼 (1037~1101)

丙辰中秋，欢饮达旦，大醉，作此篇，兼怀子由。

明月几时有？
把酒问青天。
不知天上宫阙，
今夕是何年。
我欲乘风归去，
又恐琼楼玉宇，
高处不胜寒。
起舞弄清影，
何似在人间？

Water Tone Prelude

Su Shi (1037~1101)

Mid-Autumn, 1076, happily drinking until dawn, I was tipsy to write this poem and miss my younger brother Ziyou, namely, Su Che.

When is the bright moon to rise?
Drinking a cup of wine, I ask the sky.
I don't know in which year is the paradise,
Up to today and tonight.
By wind I'd like to go to the sky,
But fear the paradise is so cold,
That I mind in height.
To dance to play with the shadow,
May not be alike in the global.

转朱阁，
低绮户，
照无眠。
不应有恨，
何事长向别时圆？
人有悲欢离合，
月有阴晴圆缺，
此事古难全。
但愿人长久，
千里共婵娟。

The moonlight turns about the red hall,
Looking down over the silky window,
The moonlight lets me sleepless on my pillow.
No need to hate the bright moon,
Don't complain it will be full soon.
Until our farewell done,
Sad, happy, farewell or reunion is man's character,
Cloudy, shiny, full or non-full is the moon's
nature,
Which means everything is incomplete.
May we keep on living a long life,
Let us share one thousand miles of moonlight.

琴诗

苏轼 (1037~1101)

若言琴上有琴声，
放在匣中何不鸣？
若言声在指头上，
何不于君指上听？

Chinese Zither Poetry

Su Shi (1037~1101)

If the music originated from the zither,
Why it was in box not to hear of music?
If the music came from player's finger,
Why you did not listen to his hand?

题西林壁①

苏轼 (1037~1101)

横看成岭侧成峰，
远近高低各不同。
不识庐山真面目，
只缘身在此山中。

Inscription to the West Cliff Surface

Su Shi (1037~1101)

Different vision angles form the different pictures,
Distant objects seem different either high or low.
Why could not see the mountain's true look,
Just because you are shut into the inside peak.

【注释】

① 这首诗有新思想，前人有过，却没人说过，苏轼说出来了。苏轼这首诗是“以议论入诗”的典范，是宋诗的一种革新。

“唐诗主情，宋诗主理”，既然要说理，就得“以文入诗”，因为诗写情，文说理；既然要说理，就得“以议论入诗”，苏轼用自己的哲理诗维护了宋诗。

卜算子

李之仪 (1048~1117)

我住长江头，
君住长江尾。
日日思君不见君，
共饮长江水。

此水几时休？
此恨何时已？
只愿君心似我心，
定不负相思意。

Divination Song

Li Zhiyi (1048~1117)

I live in the Yangtze River's original,
You live in the Yangtze River's tail.
Day by day, I'm too lovesick to see you,
We drink the same river water, though.

When to stop flowing is the river?
When my lovesickness will be over?
I wish your heart to be like my heart,
I will never live up you to be apart.

鹊桥仙

秦观 (1049~1100)

纤云弄巧，
飞星传恨，
银汉迢迢暗渡。
金风玉露一相逢，
便胜却人间无数。

柔情似水，
佳期如梦，
忍顾鹊桥归路。
两情若是久长时，
又岂在朝朝暮暮？

The Magpie-Bridge Legend

Qin Guan (1049~1100)

The Weaving-Girl with skillful fingers was clever,
As if gentle clouds were flying faster and faster.
Silently the Cowboy-Star crossed the Milky Way,
for releasing her grief on the Double-Seventh-Day*,
Like Golden Wind and Jade Dew merged once again,
No meeting was happier than the couple's reunion.

Their water-like tenderness was pretty warm,
Their reunion date's like a wonderful dream.
Weaving-Girl and Cowboy were reluctant to be apart,
The two heavenly stars knew true love would ever last,
Regardless of their mutual separation day and night.

* Chinese Double-Seventh-Day is similar to the Valentine's Day in the West.

織女
鸞梭停織歎無音夢憶仙郎夜夜心難寫
相逢容易別銀河爭似妾愁深 馬駘

一剪梅

李清照 (1084~1155)

红藕香残玉簟秋，
轻解罗裳，独上兰舟。
云中谁寄锦书来?
雁字回时，月满西楼。

花自飘零水自流，
一种相思，两处闲愁。
此情无计可消除，
才下眉头，却上心头。

A Blooming Plum

Li Qingzhao (1084~1155)

The fragrant red lotuses have withered away,
My jade-like mat turns cool on autumn day,
Lightly putting off my skirt or silky coat,
Alone I boarded on the pretty boat.
Who's to send me a letter through clouds' sky?
Looking back, the wild geese fly,
My west chamber window's full of moonlight.

Flowers drift alone out of the smell,
The creek running alone is natural.
There's one kind of lovesickness,
Coming from two places with sadness.
No way could cure such a sickness,
Just falling down from my eyebrows,
Into my heart with sorrows.

声声慢

李清照 (1084~1155)

寻寻觅觅，
冷冷清清，
凄凄惨惨戚戚。
乍暖还寒时候，
最难将息。
三杯两盏淡酒，
怎敌他、晚来风急？
雁过也，
正伤心，
却是旧时相识。

满地黄花堆积，
憔悴损，
如今有谁堪摘？
守着窗儿，
独自怎生得黑？
梧桐更兼细雨，
到黄昏、点点滴滴。
这次第，
怎一个愁字了得！

Tone Slowly Slowing down

Li Qingzhao (1084~1155)

To seek, seek, and search again silently,
I feel cold, cold, and lonely again quietly,
Chilly, chilly, and unhappy and gloomy.
Suddenly it's getting warm but still cold,
Keeping fit for me was difficult.
Two or three cups of soft wine,
Could stop speedy wind at night?
The flying wild geese in a line,
As my old friends in the sky,
Being sad, I'm heartbroken with a sigh.

The ground full of flowers in yellow,
The withered were wan and sallow,
Who would like to pick?
I had to guard my window,
How lonely could I stay after dark?
The parasol leaves were clicked by the drizzle,
Drop-by-drop at dusk.
Such a series of clicking the tonal,
Could be summed up by a word "sorrow"?

如梦令

李清照 (1084~1155)

昨夜雨疏风骤，
浓睡不消残酒。
试问卷帘人，
却道海棠依旧。
知否？知否？
应是绿肥红瘦。

As a Dream Verse

Li Qingzhao (1084~1155)

Last night it drizzled and was suddenly windy,
A deep sleep later, was I still tipsy.
Opening the roller blind, the maid told so:
"The crabapple blossoms as usual."
You know? You know?
The green is more, the red few.

如梦令

李清照 (1084~1155)

常记溪亭日暮，
沉醉不知归路。
兴尽晚回舟，
误入藕花深处。
争渡，争渡，
惊起一滩鸥鹭。

As a Dream Verse

Li Qingzhao (1084~1155)

The Water Pavilion sunset often in dream,
Deeply intoxicated, we lost our way home.
Enjoying fully, we returned late by boat,
Taking a wrong road where lotuses grow.
Paddle, paddle!
Egrets and gulls suddenly fly in a row.

点绛唇

闺思

李清照 (1084~1155)

寂寞深闺，
柔肠一寸愁千缕。
惜春春去，
几点催花雨。

倚遍阑干，
只是无情绪！
人何处？
连天衰草，
望断归来路。

Lip Painted in Crimson

Li Qingzhao (1084~1155)

My own boudoir lonely,
One piece of my heart broken, one thousand piece
sorrows remain.
I have no way to keep spring to stay,
Some raindrops promote flowers to fall away.

It's the balustrade leaning upon,
I'm in no good spirits but depression.
Where is my man?
Weak grass spreading to the skyline's goal,
My eyes failed to see his way home.

乌江①

李清照 (1084~1155)

生当作人杰，
死亦为鬼雄。
至今思项羽，
不肯过江东。

Wujiang River

Li Qingzhao (1084~1155)

You live, you must be outstanding,
You die, you must be a ghost king.
Xiang Yu*, up to now, still I miss you,
Not cross the river east but you hero.

【注释】

① 此诗因版本不同，题目又作《绝句》或《夏日绝句》。公元 1127 年（靖康二年），金兵入侵中原，掳走徽、钦二帝，赵宋王朝被迫南逃。李清照之夫赵明诚出任建康知府。城中爆发叛乱，他不思平叛，临阵脱逃。李清照为国为夫感到耻辱，在路过乌江时，有感于项羽的悲壮，创作此诗。

* As a well-known ancient brave general, Xiang Yu (232BC~202BC) killed himself when he was finally defeated near the Wujiang River.

虞姬
玉帳聞歌霸業荒蛾眉相對色
淒涼八千子弟過何處一劍空留吊項王
公周路畫於海上客次

满江红

岳飞 (1103~1142)

怒发冲冠，凭阑处，
潇潇雨歇。
抬望眼，仰天长啸，
壮怀激烈。
三十功名尘与土，
八千里路云和月。
莫等闲，白了少年头，
空悲切。

The River is Full of Blood Redness

Yue Fei (1103~1142)

My angry hair prop my hat up,
While pattering rain is to stop,
I am leaning against a railing.
Looking up at the sky,
With my loud cry,
Out of my strong desire.
I am 30 years old,
Achieving nothing well-known.
Though my eight thousand milc marching forward
on,
Under the sky with clouds and the moon.
Don't wait for nothing,
Till my grey hair's growing,
Just with my sad thing.

靖康耻，犹未雪；
臣子恨，何时灭？
驾长车，踏破贺兰山缺。
壮士饥餐胡虏肉，
笑谈渴饮匈奴血。
待从头，收拾旧山河，
朝天阙。

Don’t let our motherland in shame,
We must give back her glorious name.
My hatred to the Hun is not tame,
Let’s harness the long warring chariot again,
Pass and conquer the Helan Mountain, to destroy
the Hun’s army men.
We brave hungry fighters eat the captive Hun,
We thirsty soldiers drink the Hun’s blood for fun.
Let’s begin to recover all of our territory,
To return to our own country.

钗头凤

陆游 (1125~1210)

红酥手，黄藤酒，
满城春色宫墙柳。
东风恶，欢情薄，
一怀愁绪，几年离索。
错，错，错！

春如旧，人空瘦，
泪痕红浥鲛绡透。
桃花落，闲池阁，
山盟虽在，锦书难托。
莫，莫，莫！

Phoenix Hairpin

Lu You (1125~1210)

A rosy hand holding a cup of wine in yellow,
The whole city is so vernal with the palace willows.
The east wind is evil, my spirit is low,
A few years of separation made me in deep sorrows.
My lovesickness' still so strong,
That's wrong, wrong and wrong.

The new spring is still the original,
My soul mate is lean and sallow,
The handkerchief helps me tearful.
Over the waterside pavilion, peach blossoms fall,
Our eternal loyalty in heart but no love letter sent at all.
No way to show you, no way, no, no.

沈园二首

陆游 (1125~1210)

一

城上斜阳画角哀，
沈园非复旧池台。
伤心桥下春波绿，
曾是惊鸿照影来。

二

梦断香消四十年，
沈园柳老不吹绵。
此身行作稽山土，
犹吊遗踪一泫然。

Two Lyrics to Shen Garden

Lu You (1125~1210)

One

The setting sun over the city, the flute song is sorrowful,
Shen Garden's lake or pavilion is not like the original.
Under a heart-broken bridge, spring waves seem green,
That was not to mirror flying lovebirds once and again.

Two

A broken dream of my sweetheart lost forty years ago,
Not floating in air is catkins of the old weeping willow.
My body will be buried in the Jishan Hill,
Seeking your footprint trace, I am tearful.

病起书怀

陆游 (1125~1210)

病骨支离纱帽宽，
孤臣万里客江干。
位卑未敢忘忧国，
事定犹须待阖棺[①]。
天地神灵扶庙社[②]，
京华父老望和銮[③]。
出师一表通今古，
夜半挑灯更细看。

【注释】

① 阖（hé）棺：盖棺，指死亡。

② 庙社：宗庙和社稷，指国家朝廷。

③ 和銮：天子的车驾。

After My Recovery

Lu You (1125~1210)

Suffering from spine fracture, I am thin and weak,
I live a lonely life like a guest at the long river bank.
Though my post's low I worry about my homeland,
No conclusion can be decided until my coffin sealed.
The gods and divinities support temples or the State,
The capital city countrymen wait for emperor's chariot.
The *Battle Table Doctrine* fit from the past to present,
I read it still carefully under the midnight lamp light.

钗头凤

唐琬 (1128~1156)

世情薄，人情恶，
雨送黄昏花易落。
晓风干，泪痕残。
欲笺心事，独语斜阑。
难！难！难！

人成各，今非昨，
病魂常似秋千索。
角声寒，夜阑珊。
怕人寻问，咽泪妆欢。
瞒！瞒！瞒！

Phoenix Hairpin

Tang Wan (1128~1156)

The world love is not so thick,
The human love is so wicked,
Flowers easily fall after a raining dusk.
The wind is dry at daybreak,
My tearful remnant kept.
I'd like to write my love secret,
Alone I lean upon my balustrade.
But that's hard, hard and hard.

Both of us are apart.
Today has not been yesterday yet,
I am lovesick, as a long swing rope goes forth and back.
The cold horn lute playing music,
The night is coming to an end.
I'm afraid one will ask why I am so lovesick,
I swallow my tears into my mind.
It's my true love that I hide, hide and hide.

生查子

元夕

朱淑真[1] (1135~1180)

去年元夜时，花市灯如昼。
月上柳梢头，人约黄昏后。
今年元夜时，月与灯依旧。
不见去年人，泪湿春衫袖。

Unripe Chaenomeles Cathayensis

The Lantern Festival

Zhu Shuzhen (1135~1180)

Last year at the Lantern-Festival night,
Flower Street was like daytime bright.
The moon was hanging over tree tops of the
willow,
For dusk appointment the young couple was to go.
This is the yearly Lantern-Festival,
The moon and lanterns were bright still.
No lovely boyfriend met me to say hello,
My spring shirt was wet with my tears' flow.

【注释】

① 也有人认为本词为欧阳修所作。

朱淑貞
客約黃昏試晚粧已拚身付野鴛鴦
身名不愛訂名愛集得新編鏡斷腸
丙寅伏日環丁子醉筆作於鐙下

丑奴儿
书博山道中壁

辛弃疾 (1140~1207)

少年不识愁滋味，
爱上层楼。
爱上层楼，
为赋新词强说愁。

而今识尽愁滋味，
欲说还休。
欲说还休，
却道天凉好个秋。

Ugly Slave
Inscription on a Cliff

Xin Qiji (1140~1207)

As a young fellow, I did not know the taste of
sorrow,
I'd like to go to the high watchtower from the low.
I'd like to go to the high watchtower from the low,
I was on purpose to say "sorrow" for writing a new
poem.

Now I know what is about thc sorrow,
But I didn't want to say what I know.
But I didn't want to say what I know,
I just talk something about the autumn cold.

摸鱼儿

辛弃疾 (1140~1207)

淳熙己亥，自湖北漕移湖南，同官王正之置酒小山亭，为赋。

更能消，
几番风雨，
匆匆春又归去。
惜春长恨花开早，
何况落红无数。
春且住，
见说道，
天涯芳草迷归路，
怨春不语。
算只有殷勤，
画檐蛛网，
尽日惹飞絮。

Catching Fish by Hands

Xin Qiji (1140~1207)

The Ci-poem was written in 1179 while the poet was drinking with his partner on the Hill Pavilion Inn on the way from Hubei to Hunan.

Still it could bear the blow in the rainstorm for
  several times ago,
Spring came in and went out in a hurry.
I love spring but hate flowers to bloom so early,
Then to be withered, innumerable.
I wish spring is not to go.
Some say,
All the fragrant grass afar will lose their way,
I complain about spring not to remain.
Only the hard-working spiders,
On the pretty eaves knit web carefully to attract
  catkins all the day.

长门事，
准拟佳期又误。
蛾眉曾有人妒。
千金纵买相如赋，
脉脉此情谁诉？
君莫舞，
君不见，
玉环飞燕[①]皆尘土。
闲愁最苦。
休去倚危楼，
斜阳正在，
烟柳断肠处。

Long-gate-palace romance was told about Queen Chen* being disfavored.
She lost her chance to be a favorite.
As an emperor's beauty, she was envied.
It was hard for her to buy a scholar Xiangru's poem,
Who could illustrate her mind full of bitter gloom?
Alas, don't dance so early.
Did you see Beauty Yuhuan or Feiyan** in suicide way?
The most bitter is out of inner sorrow freely.
Don't step on the higher watchtower in sorrow.
As the setting sun was to fall with the evening glow,
I'm heart-broken under the misty willow.

【注释】

① 玉环飞燕：赵飞燕是汉成帝刘骜的第二任皇后，受成帝专宠近十年，贵倾后宫，在中国历史上是传奇的人物和神话般的美女。所谓"环肥燕瘦"讲的便是她和杨玉环。

* Queen Chen here refers to Chen Ajiao as the first wife of Emperor Liu Che. However years later she was disfavored to live in the so-called imperial Cold-Palace.

** Zhao Feiyan was the Han Dynasty's Emperor Liu Ao's queen, and Yang Yuhuan was the Tang Dynasty's Emperor Li Longji's concubine. Both of them were well-known beauties in Chinese history.

姑苏怀古

姜夔[1] (1155~1221)

夜暗归云绕柁牙[2]，
江涵星影鹭眠沙。
行人怅望苏台[3]柳，
曾与吴王扫落花。

Nostalgia to Gusu

Jiang Kui (1155~1221)

At dark night, around the river boat, rapid clouds
were to flow,
Egrets slept at sandy beach, waters swallowed
stars' shadow.
The melancholy pedestrians watched willows at
Gusu Pavilion,
Which used to accompany King Wu to sweep
flowers fallen.

【注释】

① 姜夔（kuí）：南宋文学家、音乐家。一生没有做过官，精音律，善诗词。他的词对于南宋后期词坛的格律化产生过巨大影响。

② 柁（duò）牙：指船柁。

③ 苏台：即姑苏台，吴王夫差与西施沉溺于歌舞之处。

无题

杨桂枝[1] (1162~1232)

薄薄残妆淡淡香，
眼前犹得玩春光。
公言[2]一岁轻荣悴，
肯厌繁华惜醉乡。

An Untitled Lyric Poem

Queen Yang Guizhi (1162~1232)

Her faint residual makeup remaining fragrant was light,
Still she had to be appreciating her spring scenery sight.
Yearly lightly-blooming season flowers would be gone,
Tired of prosperity, I treasured my tipsy hometown.

【注释】

① 杨桂枝：南宋宁宗皇后，出身低微，乾道年间，随养母入宫当杂剧演员；因容貌出众，受到宁宗宠爱，被册封为贵妃。为在深宫立足，她认同乡杨次山为兄，以“杨”为姓，自称“杨妹子”。

② 公言：公开谈论。

题临安邸

林升 (1163~1189)

山外青山楼外楼，
西湖歌舞几时休。
暖风熏得游人醉，
直把杭州作汴州。

Inscription to the Official Mansion

Lin Sheng (1163~1189)

One mountain follows after another mountain,
  one pavilion stands after another pavilion,
Singing and dancing went on without break,
  around the wonderful area of the West Lake.
The warm wind blowing, officials were tipsy,
They prefer to flee than to recover capital city.

约客

赵师秀 (1170~1219)

黄梅时节家家雨，
青草池塘处处蛙。
有约不来过夜半，
闲敲棋子落灯花。

A Date with My Guest

Zhao Shixiu (1170~1219)

In the rainy season, every family are in the rain,
In the grass pond, frogs croak time and again.
My date guest has not come in after midnight,
Leisurely I click chess to fall fire-pans out of light.

偶题

张良臣 (约1174年前后在世)

谁家池馆静萧萧，
斜倚朱门不敢敲。
一段好春藏不住，
粉墙斜露杏花梢。

Extempore Verse

Zhang Liangchen (before or after 1174)

Standing still to keep silent is the private waterside
  pavilion,
Leaning upon it, I dare not knock at the gate in
  vermilion.
It is impossible to hide the spring scenery at all,
As some apricot twigs dance over the painting wall.

庚辰西域清明

耶律楚材 (1190~1244)

清明时节过边城，
远客临风几许情。
野鸟间关难解语，
山花烂熳不知名。
蒲萄酒熟愁肠乱，
玛瑙杯寒醉眼明。
遥想故园今好在，
梨花深院鹧鸪声。

On Memorial Day in 1240, in the West Frontier

Yelü Chucai (1190~1244)

Passing by the frontier on Memorial Day,
As a remote guest, I was welcome cordially.
The Pass cannot illustrate the wild birds' singing,
The hilly nameless flowers were in vivid blooming.
The grape-brewed wine got me melancholy,
Cold bright agate cup puzzled my eyes tipsy.
I'd like imaging good views of my hometown,
That pear-blooming yard blocked the partridge song.

游园不值①

叶绍翁 (1194~?)

应怜屐齿②印苍苔，
小扣柴扉久不开。
春色满园关不住，
一枝红杏出墙来。

Failure in Visiting the Garden

Ye Shaoweng (1194~?)

My clogs hesitated to touch the moss in green,
The door was clicked much longer, not open.
Spring air's too overfull to be shut in the garden,
Over the wall was one red apricot-twig to span.

【注释】

① 不值：没有得到机会。

② 屐（jī）齿：屐指木底鞋，鞋底前后的高跟叫屐齿。

大德歌

关汉卿 (1234~1300)

风飘飘，雨潇潇，
便做陈抟也睡不着。
懊恼伤怀抱，
扑簌簌泪点抛。
秋蝉噪罢寒蛩儿叫，
淅零零细雨打芭蕉。

Grand Morality (Qu-Verse)

Guan Hanqing (1234~1300)

The wind whistling, the rain is pattering,
I could hardly be sleeping, even if I took Chen
  Tuan* as an example.
Still my mind is full of regretful trouble,
My tears continuously fall.
When cicadas stopped noising, crickets are singing,
On the palm the drizzle is clicking.

* It was told in the Five Dynasties (907~960), Taoist Chen Tuan was addicted to sleep soundly for 100 days and nights.

过零丁洋①

文天祥 (1236~1283)

辛苦遭逢起一经，
干戈寥落四周星。
山河破碎风飘絮，
身世浮沉雨打萍。
惶恐滩头说惶恐，
零丁洋里叹零丁。
人生自古谁无死？
留取丹心照汗青。

【注释】

① 1278年，文天祥被元军所俘，囚于零丁洋的战船中。次年正月，元军攻打崖山，逼迫文天祥招降坚守崖山的宋军统帅张世杰。于是，文天祥写下了这首诗。

On the Lonely-Sea Warship

Wen Tianxiang (1236~1283)

My bitter sufferings' from my mastering a classic principle,
No well-equipped troops' with low morale four years ago.
Gone with the catkins, my motherland lost piece by piece,
As rain beating on duckweeds, I waved ups and downs.
The Terrified-Beach battlefield was told to my surprise.
The Lonely-Sea warship sighed with my lonely sigh.
No one could escape from the death in human life,
In China's history my hearty loyalty would shine.

阳春曲

姚燧 (1238~1313)

笔头风月时时过，
眼底儿曹渐渐多。
有人问我事如何？
人海阔，
无日不风波。

Sunny Spring Song (Qu-Verse)

Yao Sui (1238~1313)

The wind and the moon go around my pen,
Before my eyes grow up my daughter and my son.
I was asked about my being done.
People's minds like ocean,
No days, no waves happen.

凭栏人
寄征衣

姚燧 (1238~1313)

欲寄君衣君不还，
不寄君衣君又寒。
寄与不寄间，
妾身千万难。

Balustrade Observer (Qu-Verse)
Sending the Winter Clothing

Yao Sui (1238~1313)

I am afraid you'll not return home, with my winter
clothing to you,
I'm afraid you'll feel cold, without sending it to you.
I hesitate to say "yes" or "no",
How difficult is to say so!

德祐二年岁旦（其一）

郑思肖[①] (1241~1318)

力不胜于胆，
逢人空泪垂。
一心中国梦，
万古下泉诗[②]。
日近望犹见，
天高问岂知。
朝朝向南拜，
愿睹汉旌旗。

On the First Day, 1276

Zheng Sixiao (1241~1318)

The ability was falling short of my wishes,
Whenever meeting my friends, I shed tears.
My mind's full of one China-Reunion dream,
That's an everlastingly flowing spring poem.
I'd like to ask the lofty vast heaven,
When our lost land will be back again.
Every morning, I pray southward earnestly,
Wishing the Han's banner to flutter freely.

【注释】

① 郑思肖：南宋著名爱国诗人。1275 年，元兵占领苏州，当时作者正在那里。1276 年正月初一，作者感念时事，写下两首诗。本诗为第一首。

② 下泉诗：出自《诗经·曹风》。原诗表达了希望国家安定的愿望，希望有贤明的君主来治理国家，关怀百姓。

落梅风[1]

别珠帘秀

卢挚 (1242~1314?)

才欢悦，早间别，
痛煞俺好难割舍。
画船儿载将春去也，
空留下半江明月。

Falling Plum Wind (Qu-Verse)

Farewell to Zhu Lianxiu

Lu Zhi (1242~1314?)

Just we have a happy time and farewell yet,
To say good-bye is extremely reluctant.
The pretty boat carries spring to be remote,
And left nothing but a half-river moon bright.

【注释】

① 曲牌名，一名《寿阳曲》。

落梅风

答卢疏斋

珠帘秀①(生卒年不详)

山无数，烟万缕，
憔悴煞玉堂人物。
倚篷窗一生活受苦。
恨不得随大江东去。

【注释】

① 珠帘秀：即朱帘秀，女艺人，才气大，名气大，与关汉卿、卢挚等元代文人常有唱和之作。卢疏斋即卢挚之号称，与珠帘秀有深交。田汉剧作《关汉卿》对珠帘秀和关汉卿之间的缠绵痴情曾有妙笔。关汉卿在《双蝶飞》中口吐真言：

"俺与你生不同床死同穴，
发不同青心同热。"

Falling Plum Wind (Qu-Verse)

Reply to Lu Shuzhai*

Zhu Lianxiu (birth and death unknown)

Numerous mountains tall, fogs are innumerable,
As an imperial academy pal, you quite are wan
and sallow.
You live a bitter life within your window.
I urgently go along with you, seemingly with the
river to flow.

* Lu Shuzhai was a bosom friend of Zhu Lianxiu who was a versatile and sophisticated artist. She was so talented and famous that great playwright Guan Hanqing had fallen in love with her according to a drama written by Tian Han (1898~1968). It was told that Guan Hanqing wrote a Yuanqu Verse entitled *Double-Butterflies-Fly* in which he sang like this:

We never share the same bedroom,
Still we can share the same tomb.
My grey hairs differ from your black,
However our two minds think alike.

天净沙
秋思

马致远 (1250~1321)

枯藤老树昏鸦，
小桥流水人家，
古道西风瘦马。
夕阳西下，
断肠人在天涯。

The Heaven Clearing out Sands (Qu-Verse)
The Autumn Lovesickness

Ma Zhiyuan (1250~1321)

The withered vine around an old tree with the raven at dusk,
Near a resident family a small bridge across a gurgling creek,
On an old road an old thin horse is against the west wind.
The setting sun is inclining westward,
My heart-broken love is at the skyline's end.

四块玉
马嵬坡

马致远 (1250~1321)

睡海棠，
春将晚。
恨不明皇掌中看。
霓裳便是中原乱。
不因这玉环，
引起那禄山，
怎知蜀道难！

Four Pieces of Jade (Qu-Verse)
Maweipo Stop

Ma Zhiyuan (1250~1321)

Like a crabapple, she was in dream,
Spring blossoms withered, not to bloom.
Emperor Li Longji took her body as a pearl in his palm*.
The Rainbow Plumage concubine was the reason.
To lead the Monarch's degeneration,
And General An Lushan's rebelling action.
In the central China, the great disorder happened all of a sudden.
The Emperor with his vanguard army had to run from Capital Chang'an to a hard Sichuan region.

* Emperor Li Longji's concubine Yang Yuhuan was good at dancing the Rainbow-Plumage dance. She was considered as a symbol of imperial degeneration.

小桃红
春

马致远 (1250~1321)

画堂春暖绣帏重，
宝篆香微动。
此外虚名要何用？
醉乡中，
东风唤醒梨花梦。
主人爱客，
寻常迎送，
鹦鹉在金笼。

Young Peach in Red (Qu-Verse)
Spring

Ma Zhiyuan (1250~1321)

Spring is to warm the hall with an embroidered
curtain,
The incense coil is curling up to the heaven.
Except the vernal, useless is the undeserved
reputation.
I am tipsy in gloom,
The east wind has awoken my pear-blossom dream.
I love my guests,
As a rule, first I say welcome, then reluctant to be
apart with them,
My parrot is still in her cage room.

金鸡报晓

朱元璋 (1328~1398)

鸡叫一声撅一撅，
鸡叫两声撅两撅。
三声唤出扶桑日，
扫尽残星与晓月。

Golden Rooster Crowing

Zhu Yuanzhang (1328~1398)

The rooster's crowing with the tail upward once,
The rooster's crowing with the tail upward again.
Crowing thrice, the sun rises over all the mulberries.
Residual stars and early moon swept out of Heaven.

我爱秋香①

唐寅② (1470~1524)

我画蓝江水悠悠，
爱晚亭上枫叶愁。
秋月溶溶照佛寺，
香烟袅袅绕经楼。

I Love Autumn Fragrant

Tang Yin (1470~1524)

I painted the blue river slowly and slowly to flow,
Love Evening Kiosk may sense maples' sorrow.
Autumn moonlight shines on the Buddha temple,
Fragrant incense smoke goes around Sutra hall.

【注释】

① 此诗为藏头诗，四行的首字上下读起来是"我爱秋香"。此诗为英译藏头诗提供了很有意义的范例，下面的英译文也巧妙地给译成了"藏头诗"。

② 唐寅：字伯虎，与祝枝山、文徵明、徐祯卿并称为明代江南四大才子。据传，唐寅于明宪宗成化六年庚寅年寅月寅日寅时生，故名。

临江仙

杨慎 (1488~1559)

滚滚长江东逝水，
浪花淘尽英雄。
是非成败转头空，
青山依旧在，
几度夕阳红。

白发渔樵江渚上，
惯看秋月春风。
一壶浊酒喜相逢，
古今多少事，
都付笑谈中。

Riverside Fairy

Yang Shen (1488~1559)

Swiftly and swiftly rolling on and on eastward is
the Yangtze River,
Wave upon wave, all historical heroes rinsed up
by the water.
But soon it would be nothing to those who won or
lost,
And still standing firm is just the mountains green
for ever,
And still more than once the setting sun is getting
redder.

The gray-haired fisherman used to stop on an
island,
Looking up at the autumn-moon against the spring
wind.
Drinking a cup of strong wine to his old friend,
Talking about events from the past to the present,
Laughing at each other by dismissing of what
happened.

观海亭

戚继光 (1528~1588)

曾经泽国鲸鲵息，
更倚边城氛祲消。
春入汉关三月雨，
风吹秦岛五更潮。
但从使者传封事，
莫向将军问赐貂。
故里苍茫看不极，
林楸何处梦魂遥。

Ode to the Sea-Watchtower

Qi Jiguang (1528~1588)

Flood later whales were not so greedy for too
much water,
To drive off evil wind out of the frontier was still
better.
Spring visited my Frontier Pass as March raining
on,
The wind blew the beach city just before every
dawn.
The messenger's news of my promotion didn't
matter,
I care no mink-uniform to be rewarded by the
emperor.
I just miss of my boundlessly invisible hometown,
Where my native forest's to hide my dream long.

马上作

戚继光 (1528~1588)

南北驱驰报主情，
江花边草笑平生。
一年三百六十日，
都是横戈马上行。

My Horseback Verse

Qi Jiguang (1528~1588)

Galloping north or south for my own national feeling,
I had no time to enjoy all the wonderful sight-seeing.
There are over three hundred and sixty days in a year,
Riding on my horse back, I carry a spear on my shoulder.

闻都城渴雨时苦摊税

汤显祖① (1550~1616)

五风十雨亦为褒，
薄夜焚香沾御袍。
当知雨亦愁抽税，
笑说江南申渐高②。

【注释】

① 汤显祖：明代大戏剧家，代表作《牡丹亭》。一些比较文学专家称其为“中国的莎士比亚”。

② 申渐高：五代时吴国的乐工。南唐开国皇帝问：“近郊有雨，都城为何无雨？”申诙谐地对曰：“雨也怕抽税吧。”汤显祖借此典故讥讽明代税重。

"Heavy Tax Yes, Light Rain No" Told in the Capital City

Tang Xianzu (1550~1616)

The emperor praised timely-coming wind and
rain,
Over his robe, nightfall burning incense ashes
remain.
He should know the rain was also worried about
tax heavy,
For it was funny to tell about Shen Jiangao's*
rainy story.

* Shen Jiangao was a performer playing ancient musical instruments in the Five-Dynasty (907~960).

石门泉

汤显祖 (1550~1616)

春虚寒雨石门泉，
远斯虹霓近若烟。
独洗苍苔注云壑，
悬飞白鹤绕青田。

The Stone Gate Waterfall

Tang Xianzu (1550~1616)

Spring cold rain falls on the Stone Gate Waterfall,
Nearby it looks like fog, and afar like a big rainbow.
Cleaning moss cliffs standing on the cloudy ravine,
The waterfall-like white cranes flies the field in green.

无题

柳如是[1] (1618~1664)

草衣家住断桥东，
好句清如湖上风。
近日西泠夸柳隐，
桃花得气美人中。

An Untitled Poem

Liu Rushi* (1618~1664)

I am a pretty plain countryside girl, near a broken
bridge is my home,
The breeze passes by the west lake, I look like a
sensational watery lyric.
I am praised by Xiling Press literati,
Even flowers benefited from my beauty.

【注释】

① 柳如是：明末清初名妓，秦淮八艳之一。本人不但工于书法，诗词也有较高造诣。

* Liu Rushi was a famous dancing girl who was good not only at singing but also at writing poems.

家书

张英 (1637~1708)

千里修书只为墙，
让他三尺又何妨。
长城万里今犹在，
谁见当年秦始皇？

Reply a Letter from Home

Zhang Ying (1637~1708)

The letter was one thousand *li* far away from my
home,
I suggested yielding three inches instead of quarrel.
Today the Great Wall's standing still firm,
Who met the First Emperor of Qin Kingdom?

春
（回文诗）

吴绛雪[①] (1650~1674)

【译者按】可以将“莺啼岸柳弄春晴晓月明”10个字，按“回文诗结构式”，即给定的语序——

1 2 3 4 5 6 7~
4 5 6 7 8 9 10~
10 9 8 7 6 5 4~
7 6 5 4 3 2 1~
拆分成四句，组合一诗如下：

莺啼岸柳弄春晴，
柳弄春晴晓月明。
明月晓晴春弄柳，
晴春弄柳岸啼莺。

【注释】

① 吴绛雪：清代女诗人，名宗爱。自幼秉承家学，聪颖多能。9岁通音律，11岁作七绝《题晴湖春泛图》。12岁时以诗入画，设色精绝，书法不同凡响，名噪一时。绘画擅长花卉、人物，兼善写生，传世画作有《梅鹊图》《落英》等。且姿容秀丽，有国色之誉。

关于此回文诗作者，其说不一，一说是明代蒋一葵，一说是乾隆和其臣子，署名天河钓叟。根据诗如其人的常识，译者倾向于吴绛雪为该回文诗的作者。

Spring
(One of Palindrome Poetry)

Wu Jiangxue (1650~1674)

Orioles sing in shore-willow to help spring glow,
To help spring glow, at dawn, moon brighten willow.
Bright moon at dawn, glow spring helps willow,
Sunny spring helps willow-shore with singing oriole.

沁园春

纳兰性德 (1655~1685)

丁巳重阳前三日，梦亡妇淡妆素服，执手哽咽。语多不复能记。但临别有云：

“衔恨愿为天上月，
年年犹得向郎圆。”

妇素未工诗，不知何以得此也。觉后感赋长调：

瞬息浮生，
薄命如斯，
低徊怎忘？
记绣榻闲时，
并吹红雨，
雕阑曲处，
同倚斜阳。
梦好难留，
诗残莫续，
赢得更深哭一场。
遗容在，
只灵飙一转，
未许端详。

Spring Immersing Garden

Nalan Xingde (1655~1685)

On the Double Ninth Day, 1677, I dreamed of my dead wife with light makeup and mourning dress, she shook my hands to weep. Her speech was too long to repeat but her farewell lyric I remembered:

I prefer to be the moon, swallowing
my sorrow,
Yearly by yearly I am willing to go
around you.

When I woke up , I wrote a long lyric verse as follows:

The floating life is like twinkling,
Life is too weak to be fleeting,
I couldn’t forget our wandering happily.
I remember quilts embroidered leisurely,
The breeze blew peach blossoms to fall.
Being slant is the carved railing,
We leant to watch the sun setting.
Wonderful dream could not remain,
My poem couldn’t be sent to you again,
What I could do was to weep in pain.
Your photo stood still,
Gone afar was only your soul.
I looked at it just a moment.

重寻碧落茫茫，
料短发，
朝来定有霜。
便人间天上，
尘缘未断，
春花秋叶，
触绪还伤。
欲结绸缪，
翻惊摇落，
减尽荀衣昨日香。
真无奈，
把声声檐雨，
谱出回肠。

Seeking for your shadow in the vast,
I imagined your hair would be like frost,
When you were back again,
We would separate between the earth and the
heaven.
Our predestined love could ever last,
The existence of spring flowers and autumn leaves
would arouse my passion.
Love ties would bind us closely till the last,
To my surprise, you passed away,
I could hardly control my deep sorrow last day.
I tried to forget my lovesickness,
However really helpless.
From eaves, dropping was the rain that composed
a song, my heart broken.

木兰花令①

纳兰性德 (1655~1685)

人生若只如初见，
何事秋风悲画扇②？
等闲变却故人心，
却道故人心易变。
骊山语罢清宵半，
泪雨霖铃终不怨。
何如薄幸锦衣郎，
比翼连枝当日愿。

【注释】

①“令”是指篇幅短小的词。但词中称“令”的，并非都是小令，如“百字令”即有百字之多。“令”也是散曲体式之一。元、明时民间流行的小曲也称为小令。

② 本句以秋扇为喻抒发被弃之怨情。南朝梁刘孝绰《班婕妤怨》诗有“妾身似秋扇”的说法。

Magnolia Flower Short Verse

Nalan Xingde (1655~1685)

If the first love was to last in human whole life,
Why Autumn-Fan* sighed herself a disfavored wife?
Nowadays a sweetheart so lightly changing her mind,
That such a frivolous attitude still considered as a style.
Once at midnight, an imperial couple sworn a love vow,
The concubine was tearful in whisper without sorrow.
Even if the heartless emperor was such a fickle guy,
Still he would swear a love oath “wing-to-wing to fly”.

* Usually, Autumn-Fan used as an analogy of disfavored beautiful lady.

予告归里画竹别潍县绅士民

郑板桥 (1693~1766)

乌纱掷去不为官，
囊橐萧萧两袖寒。
写取一枝清瘦竹，
秋风江上作渔竿。

Painting a Bamboo as a Prediction to Home Again

Zheng Banqiao (1693~1766)

Not to be an official, the black-gauze hat I throw,
An empty sack carried on my arms with sleeves
cold.
I paint a thin bamboo to stand in light of shadow,
It will be used on the autumn river as a fishing rod.

枉凝眉

曹雪芹 (1715~1763)

一个是阆苑仙葩，
一个是美玉无瑕。
若说没奇缘，
今生偏又遇着他；
若说有奇缘，
如何心事终虚化？

一个枉自嗟呀，
一个空劳牵挂，
一个是水中月，
一个是镜中花。
想眼中能有多少泪珠儿，
怎禁得秋流到冬尽，
春流到夏！

Melancholy Eyeballing in Vain (Qu-Verse)

Cao Xueqin (1715~1763)

One is a fairy flower in garden,
The other is a flawless jade in green.
If not predestined,
Why did they meet again?
If predestined,
Why their romance broken?

One is powerlessly to sigh,
The other is sympathetic in vain.
One is like the moon in the water,
The other is a flower in the mirror.
Imagine how long tears will flow?
Why their tears always drop with sorrows,
As four seasons come and go?

终身误

曹雪芹 (1715~1763)

都道是金玉良姻，
俺只念木石前盟。
空对着，山中高士晶莹雪，
终不忘，世外仙姝寂寞林。
叹人间，美中不足今方信。
纵然是齐眉举案，
到底意难平。

Lifelong Regret (Qu-Verse)

Cao Xueqin (1715~1763)

All say our marriage means a Gold-Jade union,
But still I recall my Wood-Stone love combination.
Vainly I glimpse a lofty hilly crystal-snowy love,
Lastly I remember a heavenly fairy lonely grove.
Alas, nothing is perfect to be believable!
Though my bride is pretty hospitable,
Still my mind is uncomfortable.

葬花吟

曹雪芹 (1715~1763)

花谢花飞花满天，
红消香断有谁怜？
游丝软系飘春榭，
落絮轻沾扑绣帘。
闺中女儿惜春暮，
愁绪满怀无释处。
手把花锄出绣帘，
忍踏落花来复去。
柳丝榆荚自芳菲，
不管桃飘与李飞。
桃李明年能再发，
明年闺中知有谁？
三月香巢已垒成，
梁间燕子太无情！
明年花发虽可啄，
却不道，人去梁空巢也倾。

Lyric at Burying Flowers

Cao Xueqin (1715~1763)

Over the sky, the withered flowers flying lightly,
Who pitied the scent lost or the red faded away?
Soft gossamers clung and floated to spring
pavilion,
Flying catkins glued to the embroidered-curtain.
In boudoir the girl had a pity on late spring,
She had no way to make gloomy mood thin.
Hoe in her hand, outside her embroidered curtain,
She was afraid of treading on flowers being fallen.
The willow sprigs or sweet elm fresh seeds grow
fully,
Regardless of either peaches or plums bloom
freely.
Both flowery trees will still bloom again next year,
But who will stay in the same maiden chamber?
A warm nest has been established in March
season,
Over beam swallows are heartless due to flowers
fallen.
The blooming flowers will be pecked again next
year,
The nest may be broken with the roomer gone
sooner.

一年三百六十日，
风刀霜剑严相逼。
明媚鲜妍能几时，
一朝漂泊难寻觅。
花开易见落难寻，
阶前闷杀葬花人。
独倚花锄泪暗洒，
洒上空枝见血痕。
杜鹃无语正黄昏，
荷锄归去掩重门。
青灯照壁人初睡，
冷雨敲窗被未温。
怪奴底事倍伤神？
半为怜春半恼春。
怜春忽至恼忽去，
至又无言去不闻。

There are three-hundred and sixty days every year,
The sword-like wind and frost will hurt each flower.
Flowers could not be fresh and bright much longer,
Once gone with the wind, they would be lost forever.
It's easier to seek for newly fresh flowers than the fallen,
Downstairs, burying the fallen, she was heartbroken.
Alone relying on her hoe, she's shedding tears silently,
Her tears turned bloodstained on the bare peach tree.
At dusk a happy-singing cuckoo had nothing to say,
Hoe in hand she was back to shut her door closely.
The lamp lightened the wall, initially she lay sleepy,
The cold rain clicking the window, the quilt was icy.
It's doubly melancholy to blame her lovesick thinking,
Partly due to spring love, partly due to vexation feeling.
She regretted love suddenly came to her but soon lost,
Love met her to say nothing and then silently left.

昨宵庭外悲歌发， 知是花魂与鸟魂。 花魂鸟魂总难留， 鸟自无言花自羞。 愿奴胁下生双翼， 随花飞到天尽头。 天尽头，何处有香丘？ 未若锦囊收艳骨， 一抔净土掩风流。 质本洁来还洁去， 莫教污淖陷渠沟。 尔今死去侬收葬， 未卜侬身何日丧？ 侬今葬花人笑痴， 他年葬侬知是谁？ 试看春残花渐落， 便是红颜老死时。 一朝春尽红颜老， 花落人亡两不知！	Last night she heard of an outside sad melody, That had to be flowers' or birds' soul-morality. It's hard for either flower-soul or bird-soul to stay, The flowers were shy and the birds had nothing to say. She wished to have her arms turn into double wings to fly, She would follow after flowers to reach the end of the sky. At the heavenly end, where is the flowery hill? It is better to pack the petals up with a brocade parcel, They would be buried in a kind of soil or gravel. The nature has given itself back to the pure, Don't let the dirty mire remain anywhere. Now you are passing away, I bury, I cannot predict when to bury my body. Someone laughs at me for my foolish burial today, Who will be an idiot to bury my corpse one day? Well, see spring remnant with flowers fading away, That's a beauty's exact date to be passing away. Spring drawing to an end, the beauty'll get old and old, The withered flowers or the dead beauty may not be told.

春夜即事①

曹雪芹 (1715~1763)

霞绡云幄任铺陈，
隔巷蟆更听未真。
枕上轻寒窗外雨，
眼前春色梦中人。
盈盈烛泪因谁泣，
点点花愁为我嗔。
自是小鬟娇懒惯，
拥衾不耐笑言频。

【注释】

① 出自《红楼梦》第二十三回。贾宝玉进了大观园后，以自己一年四季与姊妹丫鬟们相亲相近的生活情景为主题写了四首诗，名为"四时即事"。本诗是第一首。

Extempore Verse at Spring Night

Cao Xueqin (1715~1763)

The cloud-like tent hung and embroidered quilt
lain,
The watchman's rattle was heard hardly across
lane.
The pillow is a little cold, the rain clicked the
window,
The spring sight visible, I dreamed of a favorite
girl.
For what reason the candle's full tears are to flow?
Being angry at me, candle's embers in a bit
sorrow.
The opinionated maid spoiled herself to be lazy,
She owned her quilt to flirt, smiling frivolously.

夏夜即事

曹雪芹 (1715~1763)

倦绣佳人幽梦长，
金笼鹦鹉唤茶汤。
窗明麝月开宫镜，
室霭檀云品玉香。
琥珀杯倾荷露滑，
玻璃槛纳柳风凉。
水亭处处齐纨动，
帘卷朱楼罢晚妆。

Extempore Verse at Summer Night

Cao Xueqin (1715~1763)

The maid tired of embroidery due to her lovely
dream long,
The parrot in golden cage was calling "making tea"
as a song.
Through clear windows, a mirror has the
moonlight pass,
The hazy chamber and sandalwood emit royal
fragrance.
From an amber cup, the wine was poured like
dews to flow,
Through a glass threshold was the cool wind in
the willow.
All the girls' skirts fluttering vividly at the water
pavilion,
Red chamber's curtain rolled up, the evening
makeup done.

秋夜即事

曹雪芹 (1715~1763)

绛芸轩里绝喧哗，
桂魄流光浸茜纱。
苔锁石纹容睡鹤，
井飘桐露湿栖鸦。
抱衾婢至舒金凤，
倚槛人归落翠花。
静夜不眠因酒渴，
沉烟重拨索烹茶。

Extempore Verse at Autumn Night

Cao Xueqin (1715~1763)

My Red-Chamber was to keep absolutely quiet,
The window curtain was washed by the moonlight.
On the moss boulder wild cranes seemed in nap,
Near the well, the leaf-dew wetted crows asleep.
On my bed the maid spread my gold-phoenix quilt,
Then she turned back, putting off her adornment.
I was sleepless and thirsty after wine at night,
Ordering the tea as the maid stirred charcoal fire.

冬夜即事

曹雪芹 (1715~1763)

梅魂竹梦已三更，
锦罽鹴衾① 睡未成。
松影一庭唯见鹤，
梨花满地不闻莺。
女奴翠袖诗怀冷，
公子金貂酒力轻。
却喜侍儿知试茗，
扫将新雪及时烹。

Extempore Verse at Winter Night

Cao Xueqin (1715~1763)

The night watchman's rattle into my romantic dream,
On pretty carpet with feather quilt, still sleepless I am.
The court's crane was seen through the pine-shadow,
There's no singing orioles but pear blossoms like snow.
In the green-sleeved overall, the poetic maid felt cold,
The young heavy-drunk lord put on his golden sable-coat.
It's my pleasure the maid knew the tea-made way,
She made tea by boiling fresh snow without delay.

【注释】

① 锦罽（jì）鹴（shuāng）衾：锦花毛毯，羽绒被褥。罽，指毛毯；鹴，指雁凫或野鸭。

元春判词

曹雪芹 (1715~1763)

二十年来辩是非，
榴花开处照宫闱。
三春争及初春景，
虎兔相逢大梦归。

A Prediction Fated to Jia Yuanchun*

Cao Xueqin (1715~1763)

For twenty years Initial Spring had told right from
wrong,
Pomegranates in bloom added the palace fresh
sight.
Three “Spring-named” girls let the best spring
bright,
As dreaming of hare replacing tiger, First-Spring’s
gone.

* As the first name, Yuanchun means Initial Spring or First Spring in Chinese.

晴雯判词

曹雪芹 (1715~1763)

霁月难逢，
彩云易散。
心比天高，
身为下贱。
风流灵巧招人怨。
寿夭多因诽谤生，
多情公子空牵念。

A Prediction Fated to Maiden Qingwen

Cao Xueqin (1715~1763)

It's difficult to see the moon after a rainy day,
It's easy for colorful clouds to scatter far away.
Her inner world is loftier than the heaven,
She's just a humble maiden.
Someone is jealous of the girl, being romantic and skillful.
She died young mainly due to malign,
The lyric guy's concern was in vain.

论诗

（其一）

赵翼 (1727~1814)

李杜诗篇万口传，
至今已觉不新鲜。
江山代有才人出，
各领风骚数百年。

On Poetry

Zhao Yi (1727~1814)

Li-Du's* poems have been recited by innumerable
people,
Now their poems are inconsiderable as fresh and
strong.
The homeland will bring a genius at some
timetable,
Each genius will be admirable for a few centuries
long.

* Li-Du here refers to the greatest poets Li Bai (701~762) and Du Fu (712~770) in the Tang Dynasty (618~907).

题遗山诗

赵翼 (1727~1814)

身阅兴亡浩劫空，
两朝文献一衰翁。
无官未害餐周粟，
有史深愁失楚弓。
行殿幽兰悲夜火，
故都乔木泣秋风。
国家不幸诗家幸，
赋到沧桑句便工。

Inscription to Poet Yishan

Zhao Yi (1727~1814)

Seeing the Holocaust disorderly rise and fall,
Two dynasties documents you collected in all.
No official title, no need to seek for others' bestow,
Afraid of losing Chu bow was a historical sorrow.
Orchid's row seemed to be sad of night fire burnt,
The ancient capital lofty trees wept for autumn
wind.
With national unfortunate, a poet had good luck.
The vicissitudes made him write the best work.

己亥杂诗[①]
（其五）

龚自珍[②] (1792~1841)

浩荡离愁白日斜，
吟鞭东指即天涯。
落红不是无情物，
化作春泥更护花。

【注释】

①《己亥杂诗》是龚自珍的组诗作品，共315首。

② 龚自珍：清代思想家、文学家及改良主义的先驱者。曾任内阁中书等官职。主张革除弊政，抵制外国侵略，曾全力支持林则徐禁除鸦片。48岁辞官南归，次年卒于江苏丹阳云阳书院。

The Fifth one of the Resignation Verses

Gong Zizhen (1792~1841)

The setting sun is slant with parting sorrow,
I whip horse to gallop afar to the east goal.
Fallen flowers are not heartless but silent,
To fertilize soil to nourish spring buds root.

己亥杂诗（其一二五首）

龚自珍 (1792~1841)

九州生气恃风雷，
万马齐喑究可哀。
我劝天公重抖擞，
不拘一格降人才。

The 125th one of the Resignation Verses

Gong Zizhen (1792~1841)

The Nine Prefects'* power relied on thundering storm,
The extreme sadness was ten-thousand horses' dumb.
I advice the heavenly god not to be in deep gloom,
Be fair to recommend talents beyond any rigid form.

* As an ancient Chinese term, the Nine Prefects refer to the whole China.

赠梁任公同年

黄遵宪 (1848~1905）

寸寸河山寸寸金，
侉离[①] 分裂力谁任？
杜鹃再拜忧天泪，
精卫无穷填海心。

My Heptasyllabic Quatrain Dedicated to Liang Qichao

Huang Zunxian (1848~1905)

An inch of land means an inch of gold valuable,
For the land carved up, who is to be responsible?
A tearful cuckoo kept on worrying for the country,
A magic bird had an ambition to dry up the sea.

【注释】

① 侉（kuǎ）离：分割。

鹧鸪天

（节选）

秋瑾 (1875~1907)

祖国沦陷感不禁，
闲来海外觅知音。
金瓯① 已缺总须补，
为国牺牲敢惜身。

Partridges in the Sky

Qiu Jin (1875~1907)

Motherland fall was of my great pain,
Abroad I sought bosom countrymen.
Cathay* must be of territorial integrity,
For her I fear no sacrifice of my body.

【注释】

① 金瓯：比喻完美的疆土，泛指国土。

* Cathay refers to ancient China.

去常德州中感赋①

秋瑾 (1875~1907)

一出江城百感生，
论交谁可并汪伦？
多情不若堤边柳，
犹是依依远送人。

【注释】

① 此诗写于1891年前后，作者叹无知己，唯杨柳多情。诗中“汪伦”援引自李白诗句“桃花潭水深千尺，不及汪伦送我情”。

On My Way to a Remote Town

Qiu Jin (1875~1907)

Leaving from my riverbank town, I was in deep emotion.
As for friendship, no one gave me more beyond Wang Lun.
The most passionate is not the dam's willow,
It's such a seeing-off man for me to say hello.

杜鹃花

秋瑾 (1875~1907)

杜鹃花发杜鹃啼，
似血如朱一抹齐。
应是留春留不住，
夜深风露也寒凄。

The Azalea

Qiu Jin (1875~1907)

The azaleas turning red, cuckoos are to sing,
Either blood or red is like the same thing.
We have no way to have kept spring stay,
At midnight the windy dews drop coldly.

剑歌

秋瑾 (1875~1907)

炎帝世系伤中绝，
芒芒国恨何时雪？
世无平权只强权，
话到兴亡眦欲裂。
千金市得宝剑来，
公理不恃恃赤铁。
死生一事付鸿毛，
人生到此方英杰。
饥时欲啖仇人头，
渴时欲饮匈奴血。
侠骨棱嶒傲九州，
不信太刚刚则折。
血染斑斑已化碧，
汉王诛暴由三尺。
五胡乱晋南北分，
衣冠文弱难辞责。
君不见剑气棱棱贯斗牛？
胸中了了旧恩仇？

Sword Song

Qiu Jin (1875~1907)

Breaking off Yandi-pedigree left an injury,
When we revenge for the feud on the enemy?
In the world no equal right but hegemony,
Eyes-broken-anger's out of China's adversity.
Let's pay heavy gold cash for our sword,
Let our sword speak instead of our word.
To give my life is as light as a feather,
Thus I'll be a true hero to be praised.
Hungry, let's eat the enemy's head,
Thirsty, let's drink invaders' blood.
I'm so proud of my chivalrous courage in Jiuzhou,
I don't believe my willing bone will be broken.
My red fresh blood has been turned into green,
The Han King's so cruel to kill the young fellow.
The Five-Hu divided Jin into the North and the South.
The polite manner and weak paper were both useless.
Did you see it was a sharp sword that could fight for bulls?
In your mind could you release your hatreds and revenges?

锋芒未露已惊世，
养晦京华几度秋。
一匣深藏不露锋，
知音落落世难逢。
空山一夜惊风雨，
跃跃沉吟欲化龙。
宝光闪闪惊四座，
九天白日暗无色。
按剑相顾读史书，
书中误国多奸贼。
中原忽化牧羊场，
咄咄腥风吹禹域。
除却干将与莫邪，
世界伊谁开暗黑。
斩尽妖魔百鬼藏，
澄清天下本天职。
他年成败利钝不计较，
但恃铁血主义报祖国。

It was possible to shock the globe before its edge
was to show,
How many years you had kept your secret
stratagem to seal?
A box of wise plots hidden was kept as a secret,
It was too difficult for me to seek for a soulmate.
At empty hills a sword could surprise night storm,
It looked like a dragon vigorously dancing in
dumb.
It glittered to shock the five lakes and four seas,
So as to make nine heavens dark and colorless.
Press my sword to care of reading historic books,
Telling us about China's wrongdoings from
traitors.
The central plains suddenly turned into a meadow,
Through China the aggressive fishy wind was to
blow.
Without sword-makers Ganjiang-Moye couple,
In the world who would drive off dark shadow?
Both killing all the demons and ghosts throughly,
And cleaning up the heaven was our nature duty.
One day success or failure, rise or fall, I don't care,
But be vigilant to hold swords to guard our
country.

日人石井君索和即用原韵①

秋瑾 (1875~1907)

漫云②女子不英雄，
万里乘风独向东。
诗思一帆海空阔，
梦魂三岛月玲珑。
铜驼③已陷悲回首，
汗马终惭未有功。
如许伤心家国恨，
那堪客里度春风。

【注释】

① 石井：作者的日本友人。索和（hè）：以诗赠人索取和诗。原韵：指用石井诗的诗韵。

② 漫云：不要说。

③ 铜驼：古代铜铸的骆驼状物，置于宫门外。陆游有诗曰："只愁又踏关河路，荆棘铜驼使我悲。""铜驼荆棘"或"荆棘铜驼"泛指亡国后残破的景象。

Follow After My Japanese Friend's Rhyme

Qiu Jin (1875~1907)

Don't say that no heroine ladies would be,
Thousands of miles alone she sailed the East-sea.
My poetic idea like a sail on the wide ocean,
I dreamed clearly of the dim moon over Japan.
The bronze-camel fell, recalling in great pain,
The sweat-blood horse's sorry for no contribution.
Unless care of the domestic and state revenge I
had,
In the vernal wind I wouldn't stay leisurely
abroad.

望大陆

于右任 (1879~1964)

葬我于高山之上兮，
望我故乡；
故乡不可见兮，
永不能忘。
葬我于高山之上兮，
望我大陆；
大陆不可见兮，
只有痛哭。
天苍苍，
野茫茫，
山之上，
国有殇。

Watching My Mainland of China

Yu Youren (1879~1964)

Oh, bury me on the top of a high mountain,
To look over my hometown again,
Oh, not to be seen,
Though I'll never forget the scene.
Oh, bury me on the top of a high mountain,
To look over my mainland,
Oh, not to be seen,
I had to cry in pain.
Alas, the sky is dark green,
The vast wild field could not be seen,
Over the mountain,
My country is in great pain.

送别

李叔同[①] (1880~1942)

长亭外，古道边，
芳草碧连天。
晚风拂柳笛声残，
夕阳山外山。
天之涯，地之角，
知交半零落。
一壶浊酒尽余欢，
今宵别梦寒。

【注释】

① 李叔同：即弘一法师，曾留学日本，后出家。《送别》是其未出家前所作的送别歌。

A Farewell Song

Li Shutong (1880~1942)

Outside a post long-bower,
Lying was an ancient road.
Green grass grew sweeter,
Spread over the skyline's end.
The flute whistle heard to be low,
The night breeze blew over the willow,
Beyond the hill, the setting sun in glow.
In the skyline or the final corner of globe,
Few bosom friends remained here as I know.
Be cheerful to drink away my sorrow,
Tonight my farewell dream might be cold.

自嘲

鲁迅 (1881~1936)

运交华盖欲何求，
未敢翻身已碰头。
破帽遮颜过闹市，
漏船载酒泛中流。
横眉冷对千夫指，
俯首甘为孺子牛。
躲进小楼成一统，
管他冬夏与春秋。

Self-Mockery

Lu Xun (1881~1936)

My canopy-luck may foretell me about my future doom,
I dare not to turn over, with head hit my wall of room.
Wearing a poor hat, I walked down the busy street,
The wine was loaded on board to sail by a leak boat.
Coldly to defy myriad hypocrites is my angry brows,
I am willing to be kids' ox, bowing my deep bows.
I'd like to hide myself in my chamber as a ruler,
Regardless of spring, summer, autumn or winter.

答客诮[1]

鲁迅 (1881~1936)

无情未必真豪杰，
怜子如何不丈夫？
知否兴风狂啸者，
回眸时看小於菟[2]。

Reply for Friendly Mockery

Lu Xun (1881~1936)

Being heartless may not be a heroic man,
A father must be sympathetic for his son.
Even a tigress is crazily howling in the gale,
Never forget to look after her young animal.

【注释】

① 诮（qiào）：讥讽。

② 於菟（wū tú）：老虎的别名。

自题小像

鲁迅 (1881~1936)

灵台无计逃神矢，
风雨如磐暗故园。
寄意寒星荃不察，
我以我血荐轩辕。

My Inscription on My Own Photo

Lu Xun (1881~1936)

My heart has no way to shield a godly arrow,
The storm does heavily darken my old home.
Cold stars are unaware of my sweet note,
To China I will have my blood to devote.

题三义塔

鲁迅 (1881~1936)

奔霆飞熛歼人子，
败井颓垣剩饿鸠。
偶值大心离火宅，
终遗高塔念瀛洲。
精禽梦觉仍衔石，
斗士诚坚共抗流。
度尽劫波兄弟在，
相逢一笑泯恩仇。

Inscription to the Memorial Pagoda

Lu Xun (1881~1936)

The thunderclap and lightning annihilated the
nestling of love,
Just a broken courtyard with a dry well left to a
hungry dove.
A noble mind rescued the dove from the burning
haply,
In Japan he built up a memorial pagoda as it
passed away.
In his dream, the bird still pecked pebbles to fill
the sea,
As if sailing fighters were fighting against billows
at no ease.
Experiencing kidnap-calamity, still we were in
brotherly unity,
Face-to-face with a smile, we would get rid of all
the enmity.

教我如何不想她

刘半农 (1891~1934)

天上飘着些微云，
地上吹着些微风。
啊！
微风吹动了我头发，
教我如何不想她？

月光恋爱着海洋，
海洋恋爱着月光。
啊！
这般蜜也似的银夜，
教我如何不想她？

水面落花慢慢流，
水底鱼儿慢慢游。
啊！
燕子你说些什么话？
教我如何不想她？

枯树在冷风里摇，
野火在暮色中烧。
啊！
西天还有些儿残霞，
教我如何不想她？

Love Song

Liu Bannong (1891~1934)

In the sky, light clouds floating,
On the land, the breeze was blowing.
Oh!
The breeze fluttering my hair,
How couldn't I think of her?

The Moonlight loves the sea,
The sea loves the moonlight.
Oh!
It's so sweet night like silver,
How couldn't I think of her?

On the surface, flowery waves flew lazily,
Under the water, fish group swam slowly.
Oh!
What did the swallow sing here?
How couldn't I think of her?

The withered trees swinging in cold wind,
The prairie fire was burning at twilight.
Oh!
The setting sun saw rosy clouds remnant over
there,
How couldn't I think of her?

断线风筝①

郭沫若 (1892~1978)

横空欲纵又遭禽，
挂角高瓴月影沉。
安得恒娥宫里去，
碧海晴天话素心。

The Line-Broken Kite

Guo Moruo (1892~1978)

The kite is highly hovering but caught low,
Over the roof, hanging is the moon shadow.
How to bring it to the moon palace inside,
To tell the truth to the blue sea and sky?

【注释】

① 本诗是郭沫若和于立忱的《咏风筝》。

再别康桥

徐志摩 (1897~1931)

轻轻的我走了，
正如我轻轻的来；
我轻轻的招手，
作别西天的云彩。

那河畔的金柳，
是夕阳中的新娘；
波光里的艳影，
在我的心头荡漾。

软泥上的青荇，
油油的在水底招摇；
在康河的柔波里，
我甘心做一条水草！

那榆荫下的一潭，
不是清泉，
是天上虹，
揉碎在浮藻间，
沉淀着彩虹似的梦。

Farewell to Cambridge Once More

Xu Zhimo (1897~1931)

Lightly, lightly I went away,
Lightly as I come on the same way.
Lightly, lightly I wave good-bye,
To the West clouds in the sky.

It's riverside with the golden willow,
That's a bride of the setting sun in glow.
Under the water, all colorful shadows,
In my mind and heart, seem to sparkle.

The green grass grow up in soft mire,
Oily in the water bottom swagger.
In the gentle waves of the river,
To be a piece of grass, I prefer!

Under the elm shade, that's not a pond,
But clear spring water.
Like a rainbow being crumbled,
Into the floating algae to form a dream in color.

寻梦？
撑一支长篙，
向青草更青处漫溯；
满载一船星辉，
在星辉斑斓里放歌。

但我不能放歌，
悄悄是别离的笙箫；
夏虫也为我沉默，
沉默是今晚的康桥。

悄悄的我走了，
正如我悄悄的来；
我挥一挥衣袖，
不带走一片云彩。

Looking for a dream?
Paddle a boat,
Leisurely to greener grass watery site.
Where the boat is full of starring light,
With a gorgeous song at night.

However, I cannot sing such a song so aloud,
Quietly I leave here means my music ode.
The summer cicada is dumb for my silence,
Let me leave Cambridge wordlessly tonight.

Quietly, quietly I am to go away,
Quietly as I come on the same way.
I'd like to have my sleeves roll down,
I'll not take a cloud to my hometown.

沙扬娜拉

徐志摩 (1897~1931)

最是那一低头的温柔，
像一朵水莲花不胜凉风的娇羞，
道一声珍重，道一声珍重，
那一声珍重里有蜜甜的忧愁
——沙扬娜拉！

Farewell

Xu Zhimo (1897~1931)

The most beautiful and gentle, is you make a bow,
Like a shy lotus against the wind cold
  with a watery shadow.
Take a good care of you,
Take a good care of you,
How sweet your voice is with your sweet sorrow!
Farewell, farewell!

就义诗

夏明翰[1] (1900~1928)

砍头不要紧，
只要主义真。
杀了夏明翰，
还有后来人。

Give Up one's Life Heroically

Xia Minghan (1900~1928)

Cutting off my head is a small matter,
Only my true belief is truly important.
Xia Minghan was killed as one man,
More people will follow after me again.

【注释】

① 夏明翰：湖南衡阳人。五四运动时任湖南学生联合会总干事，曾任全国农民协会秘书长。大革命失败后，领导平江农民起义。后被国民党反动派逮捕杀害。临刑前写下这首诗。

述志

袁晓园[1] (1901~2003)

夕阳未必逊晨曦，
昂首飞鬃奋老蹄。
春蚕萦绕千千缕，
愿为人民吐尽丝。

A Verse on My Will

Yuan Xiaoyuan (1901~2003)

The sunset is not inferior to the early morning,
An old horse flutters long manes, fast galloping.
Spring silkworms wound up silks long and long,
Serving the people is my will, never stopping.

【注释】

① 袁晓园：我国第一位女外交官，善诗词、书画，著作有《晓园作品选》等。

你是人间的四月天
——一句爱的赞颂

林徽因（1904~1955）

我说你是人间的四月天；
笑响点亮了四面风；
轻灵在春的光艳中交舞着变。
你是四月早天里的云烟，
黄昏吹着风的软，
星子在无意中闪，
细雨点洒在花前。

You Were My Human April-Day
— My Lovely Praise to You

Lin Huiyin (1904~1955)

In my Spring World, let me say you were my
human April-day,
You smile at the free wind lightly and lively.
The sunshine was in dancing alternatively.
You were of the cloudy mist in the early April,
The gentle wind was blowing at dusk in the
vernal,
Stars were glistering without any goal.
In front of flowers, sprinkling was the drizzle.

那轻，那娉婷，你是，
鲜妍百花的冠冕，你戴着，
你是天真，庄严，你是夜夜的月圆。
雪化后那片鹅黄，你像；
新鲜初放芽的绿，你是；
柔嫩喜悦，
水光浮动着你梦期待中白莲。
你是一树一树的花开，
是燕在梁间呢喃，——你是爱，是暖，
是希望，你是人间的四月天！

So light, so graceful, were you!
Everywhere was fresh and beautiful.
That 100-flower-crown you wore was of
the royal.
Really were you,
Naive, dignified, you seem like the full moon,
That shines every night through my window.
After snow melt, you seemed to be in light
yellow,
And also you were freshly green,
tender and joyful,
As water light fluctuating in a dream,
You long for a white lotus blooming to you.
You seemed to be trees with blossoms or
some swallows.
My porch was with your twittering, love
and warmth from you.
You were my human April-day, you were
my hope!

雨巷

戴望舒 (1905~1950)

撑着油纸伞，
独自彷徨在悠长、悠长
又寂寥的雨巷，
我希望逢着
一个丁香一样地
结着愁怨的姑娘。

她是有
丁香一样的颜色，
丁香一样的芬芳，
丁香一样的忧愁，
在雨中哀怨，
哀怨又彷徨；
她彷徨在这寂寥的雨巷。

撑着油纸伞
像我一样，
像我一样地
默默彳亍[1]着，
冷漠，凄清，又惆怅。

Rain Lane

Dai Wangshu (1905~1950)

My umbrella being unfolded on,
Along the lane, narrow but long,
Alone I was wandering down,
I longed to meet
A bitter lilac-like girl,
She's in resentful sorrow.

She was such a girl:
In lilac-like color,
With lilac-like smell,
She behaves in the lilac-like gloomy style.
She was sad in raining,
Walking back and forth, walking...
Walking down the lonely lane.

She upheld the umbrella-shaft
As I did,
As I did along the narrow lane
To be silent,
Lonely, melancholy, indifferent.

【注释】

① 彳亍（chì chù）：小步慢走的样子。

她静默地走近
走近，又投出
太息一般的眼光。
她飘过
像梦一般地，
像梦一般地凄婉迷茫。

像梦中飘过
一枝丁香地，
我身旁飘过这女郎；
她静默地远了，远了，
到了颓圮的篱墙，
走尽这雨巷。

在雨的哀曲里，
消了她的颜色，
散了她的芬芳，
消散了，甚至她的
太息般的眼光，
丁香般的惆怅。

撑着油纸伞，独自
彷徨在悠长，悠长
又寂寥的雨巷，
我希望飘过
一个丁香一样地
结着愁怨的姑娘。

In silence she was approaching,
On and on, approaching,
Glancing and glancing.
She's passing by my side gently.
I could see her as if dreaming of fancy.
Leaving me coldly, she looks vast and hazy.

Like a lilac floating lightly,
Into my dream is the lady.
Gently passing by me,
Far, far away, she was vanishing silently,
To the end of the narrow way,
In which a ruined fence lay.

Her sad rainy song,
Or her pale face with her feeling down,
Her fragrance was not strong.
Even her sighing eyesight,
Not so bright, but disconsolate.

Unfolding my umbrella, alone,
The lonesome rain-lane long, long,
I wandered on, feeling down.
I longed to see a lilac girl,
Gently on her go,
She's in resentful sorrow.

老马

臧克家 (1905~2004)

总得叫大车装个够，
它横竖不说一句话，
背上的压力往肉里扣，
它把头沉重地垂下！

这刻不知道下刻的命，
它有泪只往心里咽，
眼里飘来一道鞭影，
它抬起头望望前面。

An Old Horse

Zang Kejia (1905~2004)

The cart always fully loaded by the cargo,
The horse said nothing with a nod show.
All the loads pressed onto his back flesh,
The old horse silently had his head low.

How about his destiny he never did know,
Tears only into his mind he was to swallow.
Raising his head to look at the forward road,
In front of his eyes, flying is a whip shadow.

汉俳①

赵朴初 (1907~2000)

一

上忆土岐翁
囊书相赠许相从
遗爱绿荫浓

二

幽谷发兰馨
上有黄鹂深树鸣
喜气迓俳人

三

绿荫今雨来
山花枝接海花开
和风起汉俳

【注释】

① 汉俳：是一种诗歌体裁，是模仿日本俳句的形式，用中文创作的小型律体诗。由已故中国佛教协会会长、著名诗人赵朴初先生首创。1980年5月30日，中日友好协会首次接待“日本俳人协会访华团”。在两国诗人欢聚一堂之际，赵朴初老先生诗兴勃发，参考日本俳句十七音，依照中国诗词传统的创作声法、韵法、律法等特点，即席赋诗一首，共三章。

The First Chinese Haiku*

Zhao Puchu (1907~2000)

One

Recall historic senior Toki,
Present to you Xu Xiang biography.
Our friendship is an evergreen tree.

Two

The deep valley orchid fragrance is emitting,
Over trees top yellow orioles heard of singing.
As if to welcome Haiku poets to be coming.

Three

Dropping down the green shade was the fresh rain,
Along with the sea-flowers, the land flowers bloom
again.
The Haiku verse of Japan was the Han Haiku's
origin.

* The Chinese Haiku is similar to China's short poem in form. Currently, it seems to be no fixed requirements but characters or words strictly limited. It may be written either in classical style of writing or the modern, either in rhyme or not, either in falling tone or in rising one. However it is characterized by brevity and deep sensation that can arouse readers to imagine in mind.

放脚时代的足印

殷夫 (1910~1931)

一

春给我一瓣嫩绿的叶
我反复地寻求着诗意

二

我初见你时
我战慄着
我初接你吻时
我战慄着
如今我们永别了
我也战慄着

Epoch Footprints of Women Feet Liberation

Yin Fu (1910~1931)

One

Spring presented me a fresh leaf in green,
I try to seek my poetic ideas time and again.

Two

When I met you at first,
I was timid a little bit.
When I kissed you at first,
I was in quiver.
Now we part forever,
I'm in shudder.

我爱这土地

艾青 (1910~1996)

假如我是一只鸟，
我也应该用嘶哑的喉咙歌唱：
这被暴风雨所打击着的土地，
这永远汹涌着我们的悲愤的河流，
这无止息地吹刮着的激怒的风，
和那来自林间的无比温柔的黎明……
——然后我死了，
连羽毛也腐烂在土地里面。
为什么我的眼里常含泪水？
因为我对这土地爱得深沉……

I Love My Native Land

Ai Qing (1910~1996)

If I were a bird,
Also I should sing by my hoarse throat:
The storm used to be striking the land,
Where rivers never stopped surging,
With our turbulent grief and indignation,
The restless wind with furious expression,
Mixed by incomparably gentle daybreak
bright,
Going through the forest sunlight.
Then I'll pass away…
With feathers and my body,
To be buried and rotten in land one day.
Why do my eyes often full of tears
silently?
For I love my native land deeply...

咏风筝

于立忱[①] (1912~1937)

碧落何来五色禽，
长空万里任浮沉。
只因半缕轻丝系，
辜负乘风一片心。

Ode to a Kite

Yu Lichen (1912~1937)

A colorful bird is flying in the lofty sky,
Freely it's rolling up and down miles high.
My kite is always fastened by a thin line,
The wind disappointed of raising the kite.

【注释】

① 于立忱：别名于佩琛，于立群之姐。曾任天津《大公报》驻日本记者，其间与郭沫若往来甚多；后来应召回国，于1937年5月自杀，年仅25岁。郭沫若曾著文哀悼。

乡愁

余光中 (1928~2017)

小时候
乡愁是一枚小小的邮票
我在这头
母亲在那头

长大后
乡愁是一张窄窄的船票
我在这头
新娘在那头

后来呵
乡愁是一方矮矮的坟墓
我在外头
母亲在里头

而现在
乡愁是一湾浅浅的海峡
我在这头
大陆在那头

My Homesickness

Yu Guangzhong (1928~2017)

During my childhood,
My homesickness was a small stamp,
To mail to my mother far away,
From which I stay.

When I grew up,
It changed into a shipping ticket,
A little bit narrow,
To help me sail meet my bride by boat.

And then,
My homesickness turned into a lower tomb.
Outside the tomb I was standing dumb,
Inside it my mother lived as her home.

But now,
My homesickness means the sea beach is shallow.
Still I am on this shore instead of the mainland
shore,
Though the sea strait is narrow.

无怨的青春

席慕容 (1943~)

在年青的时候
如果你爱上了一个人
请你一定要温柔地对待她
不管你们相爱的时间有多长或多短
若你们能始终温柔地相待　那么
所有的时刻都将是一种无瑕的美丽
若不得不分离
也要好好地说一声再见
也要在心里存着感谢
感谢她给了你一份记忆
长大了之后　你才会知道
在蓦然回首的一刹那
没有怨恨的青春　才会无遗憾
如山岗上那静静的晚月

The Youth with No Resentment

Xi Murong (1943~)

A little bit young were you,
Falling in love with a girl,
Be kind to her, please do so.
Whether you love each other long or short,
Both of you ought to treasure the love at first.
All the love experience will be flawlessly beautiful.
If you had to separate from her,
You should say good-bye in a polite manner,
You should have good memories of her,
Be grateful to her forever.
One day you grow old, you should be no regret without resentful sigh,
While recalling what happened to you,
Like a peaceful moon over hills at night.

致橡树

舒婷 (1952~)

我如果爱你——
绝不像攀援的凌霄花，
借你的高枝炫耀自己；
我如果爱你——
绝不学痴情的鸟儿，
为绿荫重复单调的歌曲；
也不止像泉源，
常年送来清凉的慰藉；
也不止像险峰，
增加你的高度，
衬托你的威仪。
甚至日光。
甚至春雨。
不，这些都还不够！

我必须是你近旁的一株木棉，
作为树的形象和你站在一起。
根，紧握在地下，
叶，相触在云里。

My Lyric to Oak

Shu Ting (1952~)

If I love you —
I don't take a creeping flower as an
  example,
To creep up and to depend on you to show.
If I love you —
I don't want just to be a singing bird of you,
Repeating the monotonous song for trees'
  shadow.
Or just to be a springhead always in flow,
Just yearly repeat the cool sense to you.
And also just to be a lofty peak to uphold
  and fame you,
Just like a dignified fellow.
Even I'll give you no more sunshine or rain
  in the vernal.
However, what I need to do is much more
  as follows.

Be kapok, I must be close to you,
As the tree's image, I must be standing next
  to you.
My root must be taken tightly into
  underground,
My leaves must be touching the sky's
  cloud.

每一阵风过，
我们都互相致意，
但没有人，
听懂我们的言语。
你有你的铜枝铁干，
像刀，像剑，也像戟；
我有我红硕的花朵，
像沉重的叹息，又像英勇的火炬，
我们分担寒潮、风雷、霹雳；
我们共享雾霭、流岚、虹霓。
仿佛永远分离，
却又终身相依。

这才是伟大的爱情，
坚贞就在这里：
爱——
不仅爱你伟岸的身躯，
也爱你坚持的位置，足下的土地。

After a blast of wind,
We must mutually express our best wishes
to say hello,
Although no one understood our speech,
Still our mutual communications would go.
You have your metal-like branches of trees,
Like knives, like swords,
And also like ancient halberds.
I have my red large flowers,
Like serious sighs,
And also like heroic torches,
But we can share cold waves, storms or
thunderclaps,
We can share the fog and the rainbow,
As if they were forever to separate me from
you,
Actually lifetime is connected with me and
you.

That's called the great love I'd like to tell
you,
That's true love between me and you.
Love —
I love not only your great stature,
But also love the occupation and the field
of you.

日记

海子 (1964~1989)

姐姐，今夜我在德令哈[①]
夜色笼罩
姐姐，我今夜只有戈壁
草原尽头我两手空空
悲痛时握不住一颗泪滴
姐姐，今夜我在德令哈
这是雨水中一座荒凉的城
除了那些路过的和居住的
德令哈……今夜
这是唯一的，最后的，抒情
这是唯一的，最后的，草原
我把石头还给石头
让胜利的胜利
今夜青稞只属于他自己
一切都在生长
今夜我只有美丽的戈壁　空空
姐姐，今夜我不关心人类
我只想你

【注释】

① 德令哈：指德令哈市。德令哈是蒙古语，意为“金色的世界”，位于青海省柴达木盆地东北边缘。

My Diary

Hai Zi (1964~1989)

Dear Sister, I am in Delingha* tonight,
Under the shroud of darkness.
Dear Sister, I only have Gobi tonight.
At the end of grassland with my empty hands,
I am too sad to hold a teardrop.
Dear Sister, tonight I am in Delingha,
A desolate raining city with few passengers at
  a stop.
Delingha…tonight.
That's only my last lyrical dream,
That's my last true prairie poem.
Return stone in its original order,
Let a victor be winner.
Tonight the barley can only belong to barley,
Let every living thing grow up naturally freely.
Tonight only I have pretty Gobi with my mind
  empty.
Dear Sister, tonight I care of no human family,
But only I miss you, only...

* Delingha is the name of municipality in Mongolian language, meaning "Golden World" located at the northeast edge of Qaidam Basin in Qinghai Province, China.

黛玉

陈晓旭[1] (1965~2007)

仙草前因未可知，
侧身红粉自清奇。
今宵听入潇湘雨，
缘会他生未有期。

【注释】

① 陈晓旭:《红楼梦》1987版电视剧中林黛玉的扮演者。晓旭已经永远离开了我们，英译她的《黛玉》一韵以缅怀思念她所塑造的至今依旧栩栩如生的黛玉形象。

Lin Daiyu

Chen Xiaoxu (1965~2007)

It's unknown if an immortal grass had her pretty,
It's clear whose cheeks appeared ruddy and rosy.
Were tonight lingering drizzle heard clearly,
No exact date to carry out her fated destiny.